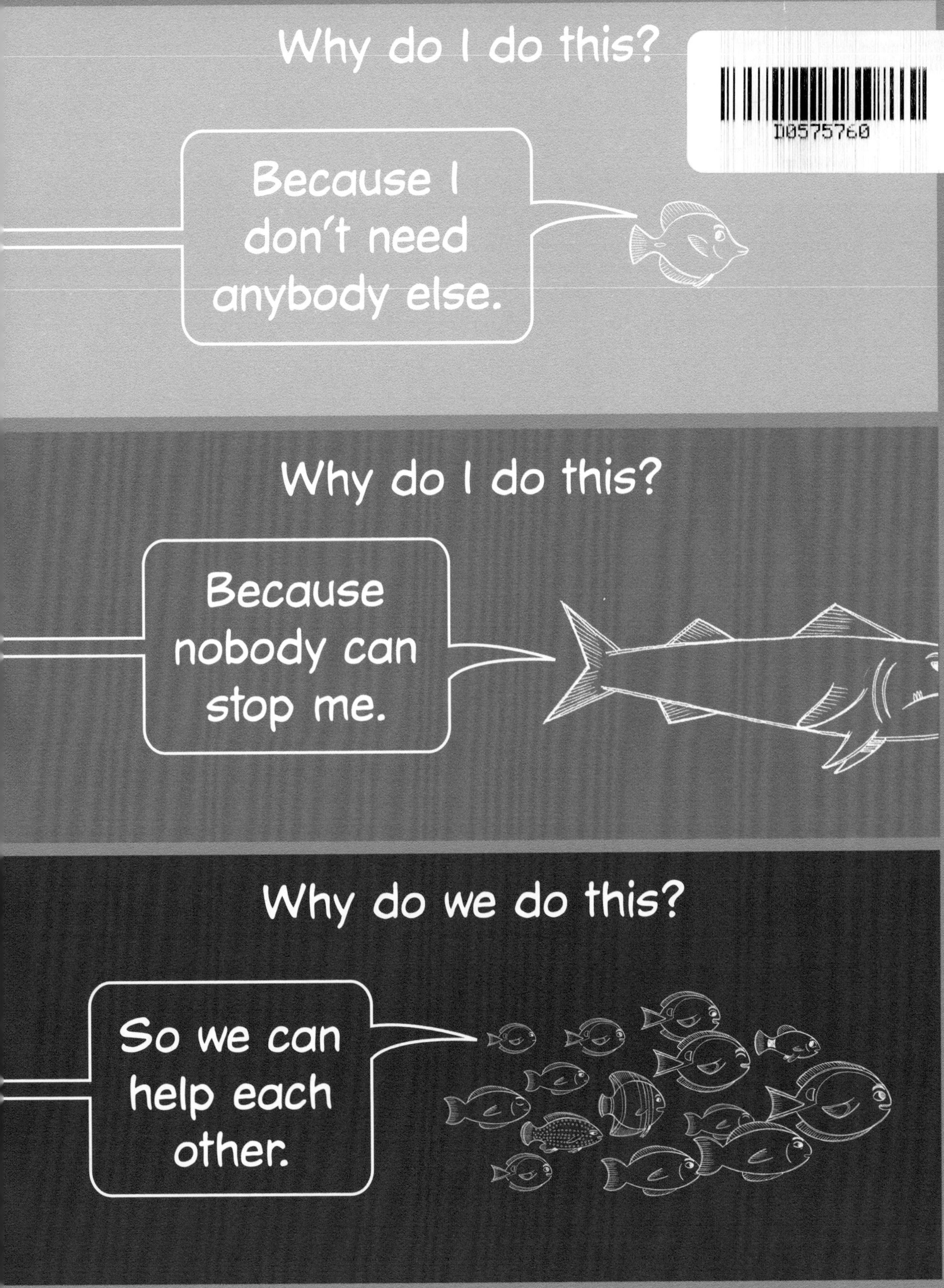
Why do I do this?
Because I don't need anybody else.
Why do I do this?
Because nobody can stop me.
Why do we do this?
So we can help each other.

...and get the whole story.

FISH FISH FISH

A GRAPHIC NOVEL

LEE NORDLING & MERITXELL BOSCH

THREE STORY BOOKS

GRAPHIC UNIVERSE™ • MINNEAPOLIS

Praise for BirdCatDog

"This innovative charmer can be read four different ways...
Stylish and inventive and an excellent examination
of point of view." –starred, *Kirkus Reviews*

"A must-own for elementary school libraries." –*School Library Journal*

For Cheri, the love of all of my lives.
And a special thanks to Andrew Karre, for embracing this vision,
as well as to Meri, for getting it right.
–Lee Nordling

This book is dedicated to Jan, my precious little boy,
and the little Leo, our new addition to the family!
Thanks to Tom for being there. To my dear friends, Pam Lopez and
Francesc Fullana, Lucia Serrano and Javi Chaler, I need you!
And especially to Lee Nordling for his infinite patience with me.
Thank you, Lee.
–Meritxell Bosch

Lee Nordling is an award-winning writer, editor,
creative director, and book packager. He worked on staff at
Disney Publishing, DC Comics, and Nickelodeon Magazine.

Meritxell Bosch is a graphic novel artist and writer, illustrator,
character designer, colorist, and art teacher, living in Barcelona, Spain.

Story and script by Lee Nordling
Art by Meritxell Bosch

FishFishFish © 2015 by Lee Nordling & Meritxell Bosch

FishFishFish and Three-Story Books were placed,
designed, and produced by The Pack.

Graphic Universe™ is a trademark of Lerner
Publishing Group, Inc.

Graphic Universe™
A division of Lerner Publishing Group, Inc.
241 First Avenue North
Minneapolis, MN 55401 USA

For reading levels and more information, look up this
title at www.lernerbooks.com.

Library of Congress Cataloging-in-Publication Data

Nordling, Lee.
 [Short stories. Selections]
 Fishfishfish / by Lee Nordling ; illustrated by
Meritxell Bosch.
  pages   cm. – (Three-story books)
 Summary: Three connected, wordless stories
relate heroic tales of a small but independent fish, a
hungry barracuda, and a school of dozens of fish.
 ISBN 978-1-4677-4575-8 (lib. bdg. : alk. paper)
 ISBN 978-1-4677-4576-5 (pbk.)
 ISBN 978-1-4677-4577-2 (EB pdf)
 1. Graphic novels. [1. Graphic novels. 2. Fishes–
Fiction. 3. Stories without words.] I. Bosch,
Meritxell, illustrator. II. Title. III. Title: Fish fish fish.
PZ7.7.N67Fis 2015
741.5'973–dc23   2014022953

Manufactured in the United States of America
1 - BP - 12/31/14

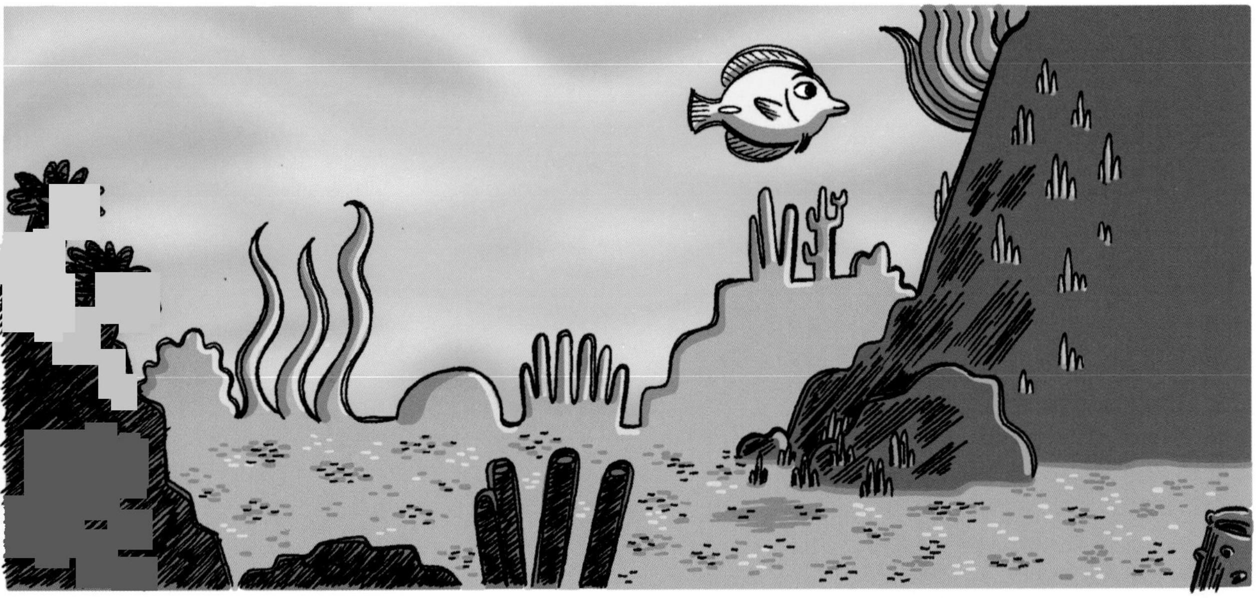

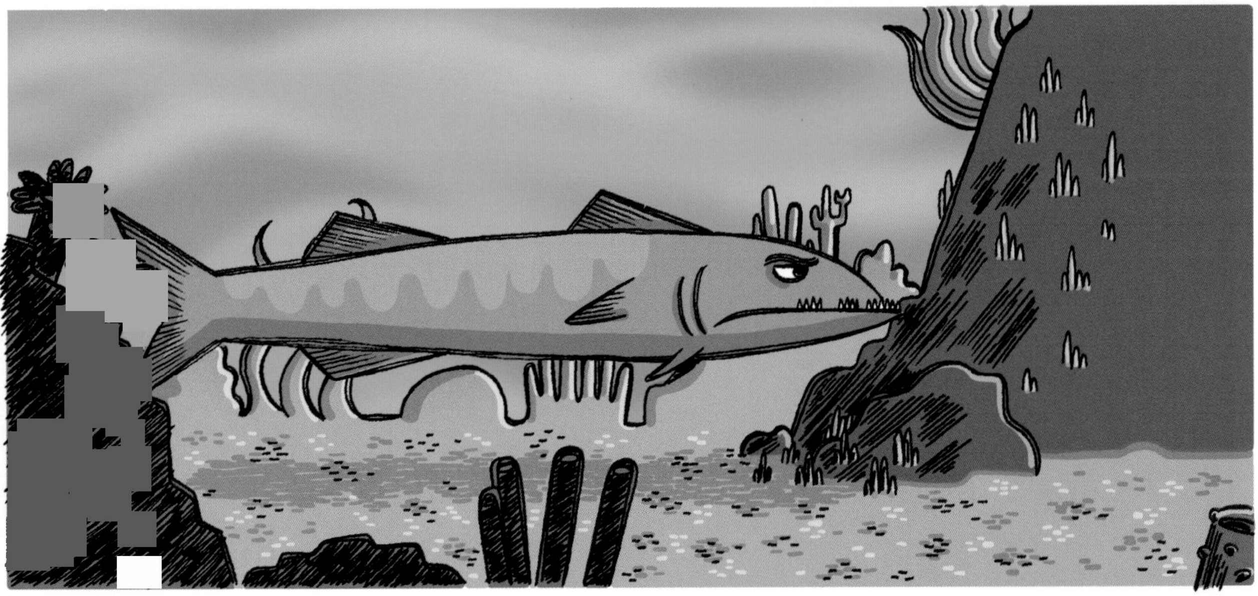

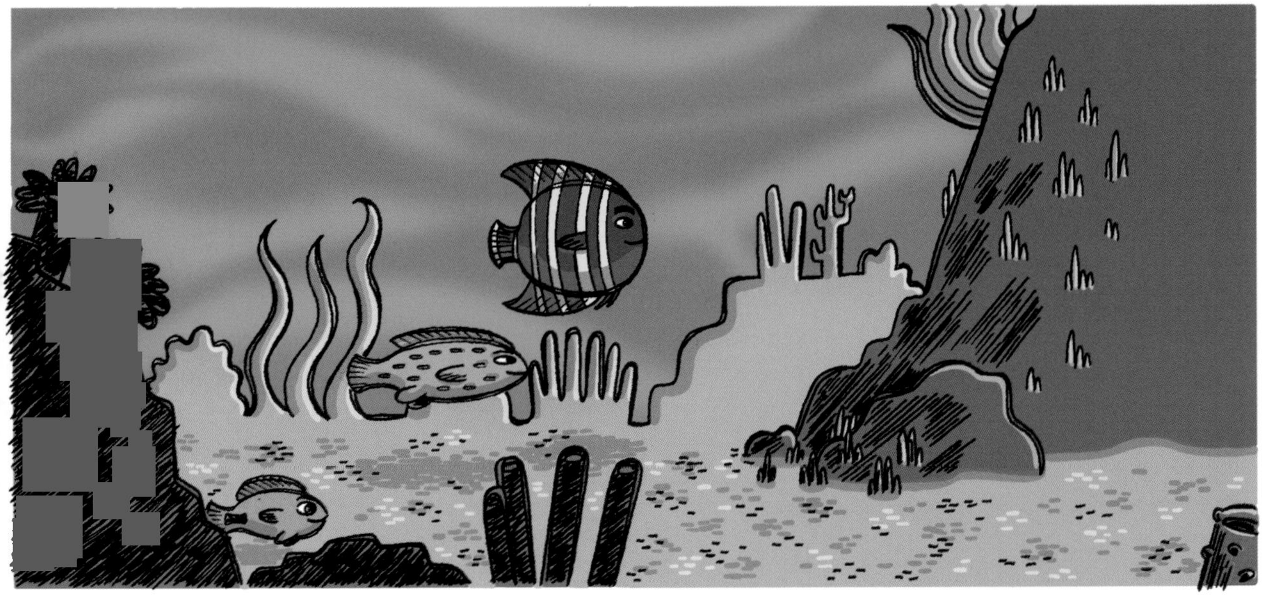

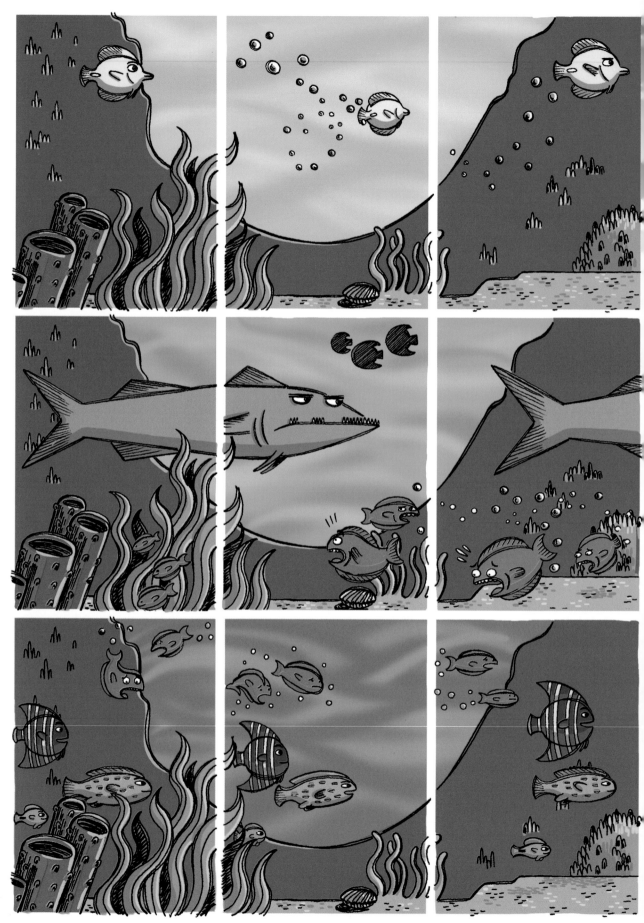

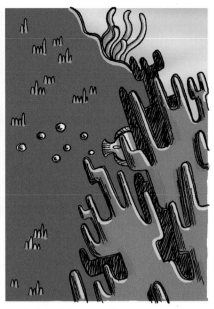

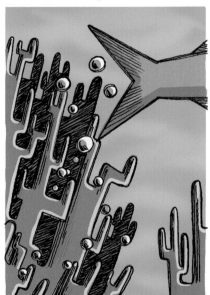

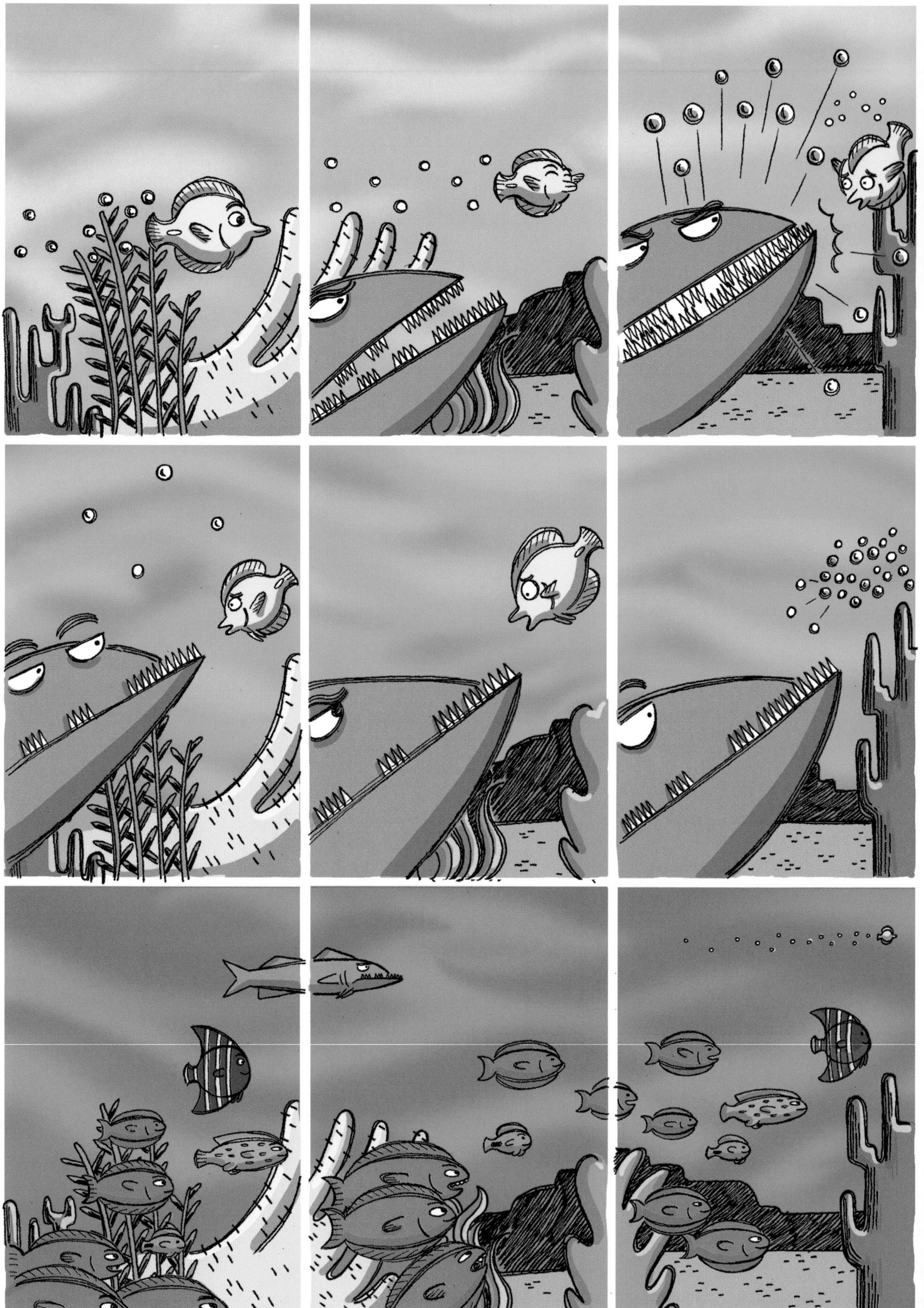

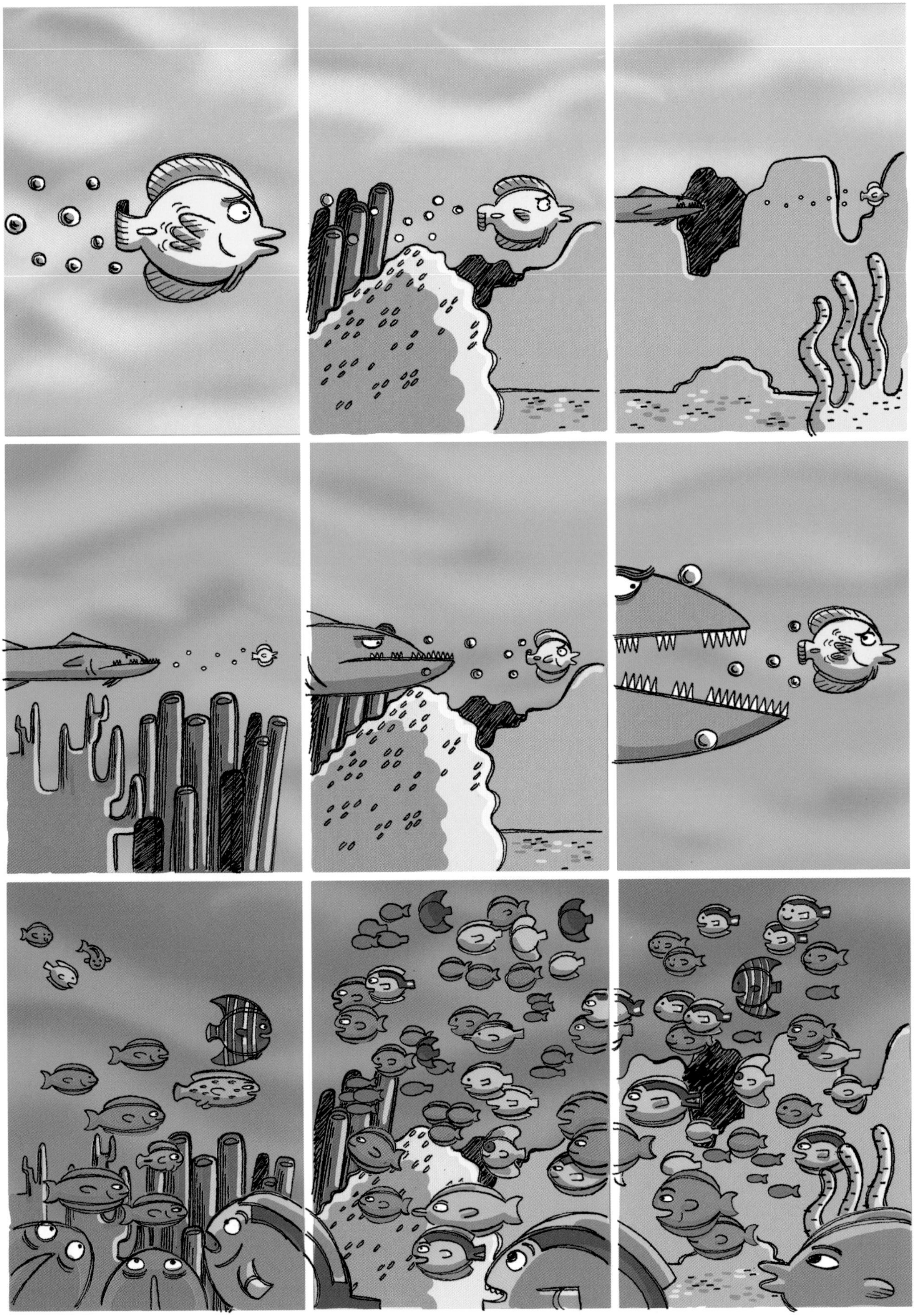

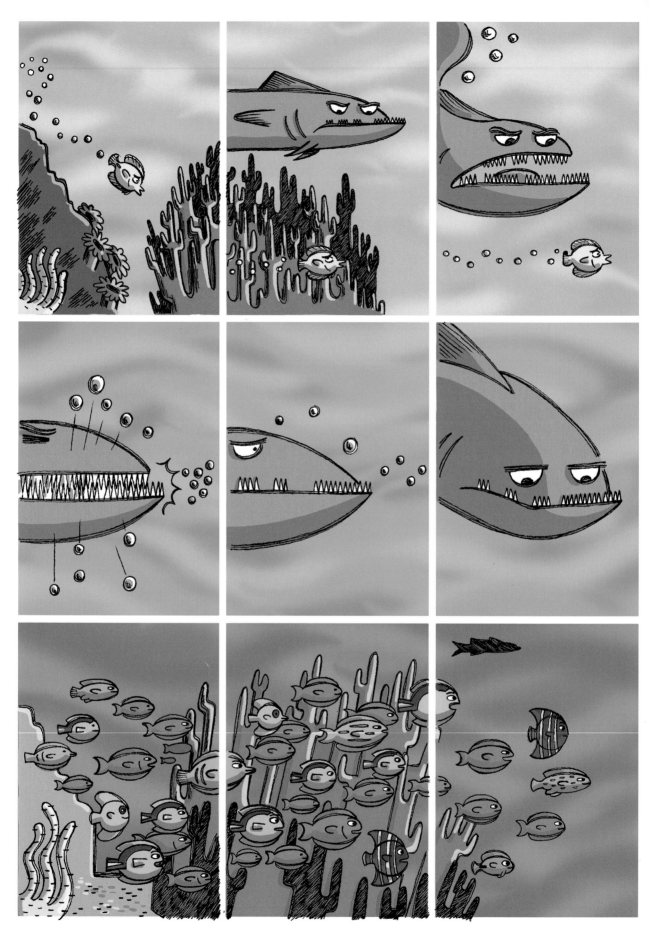

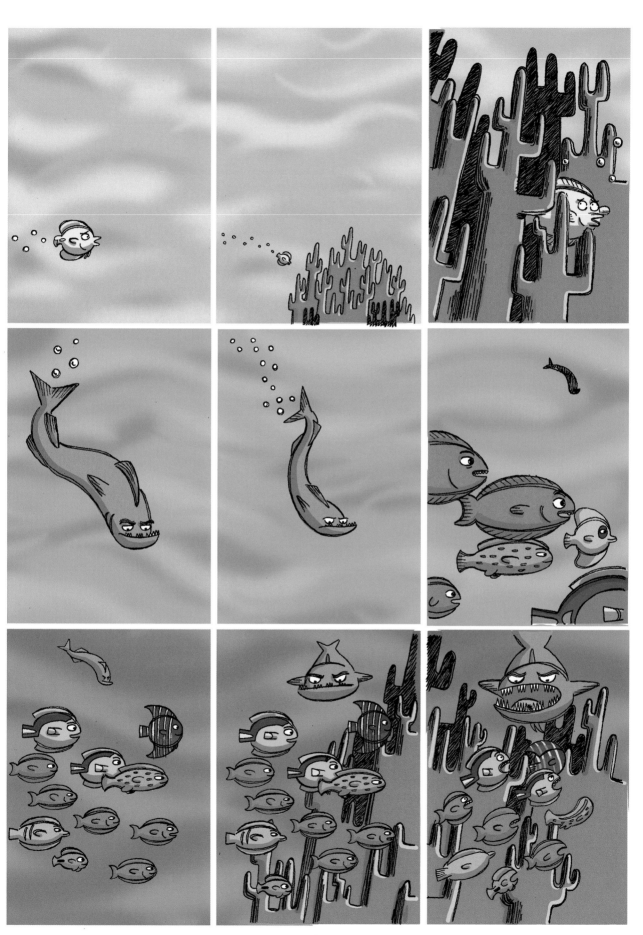

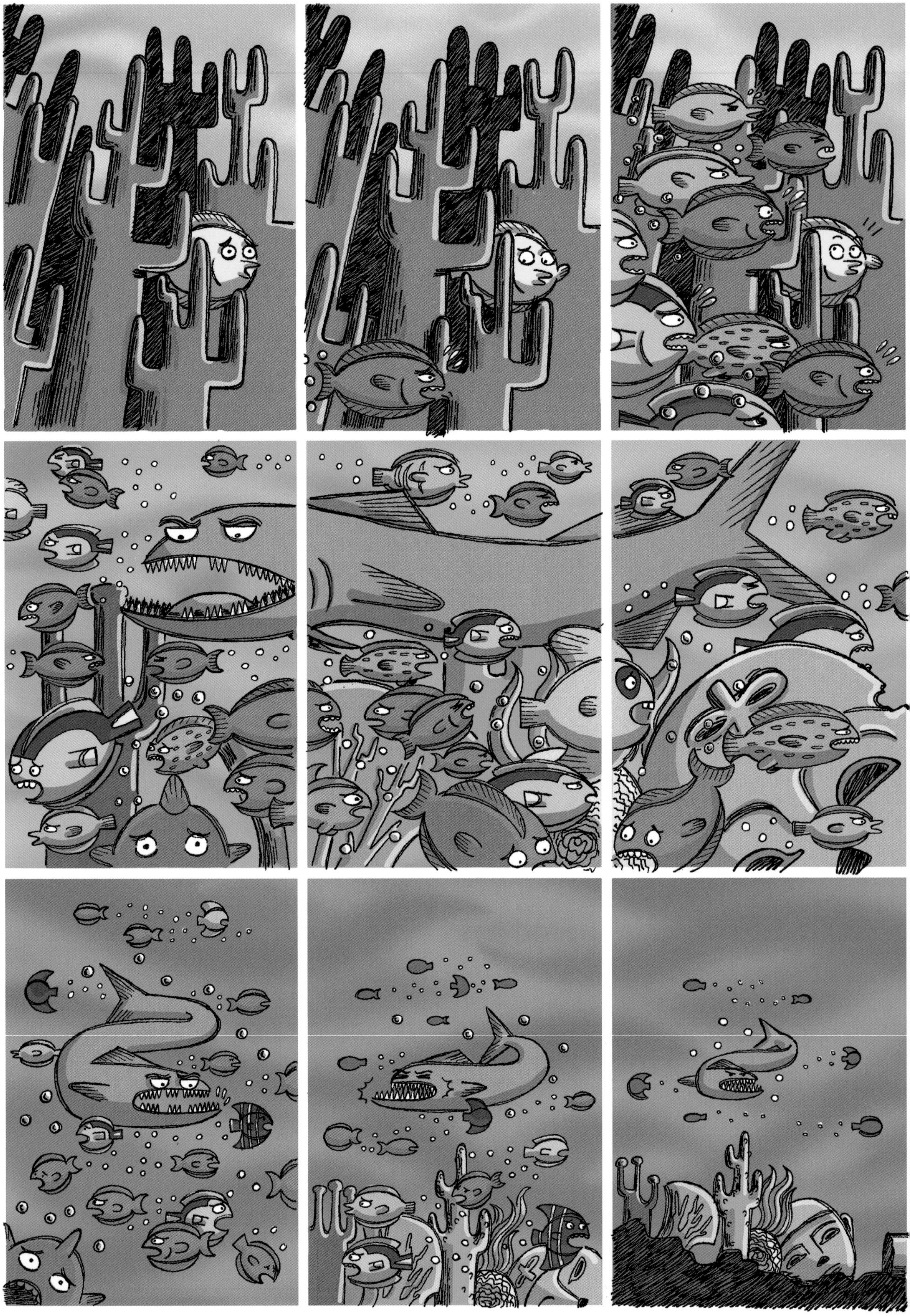

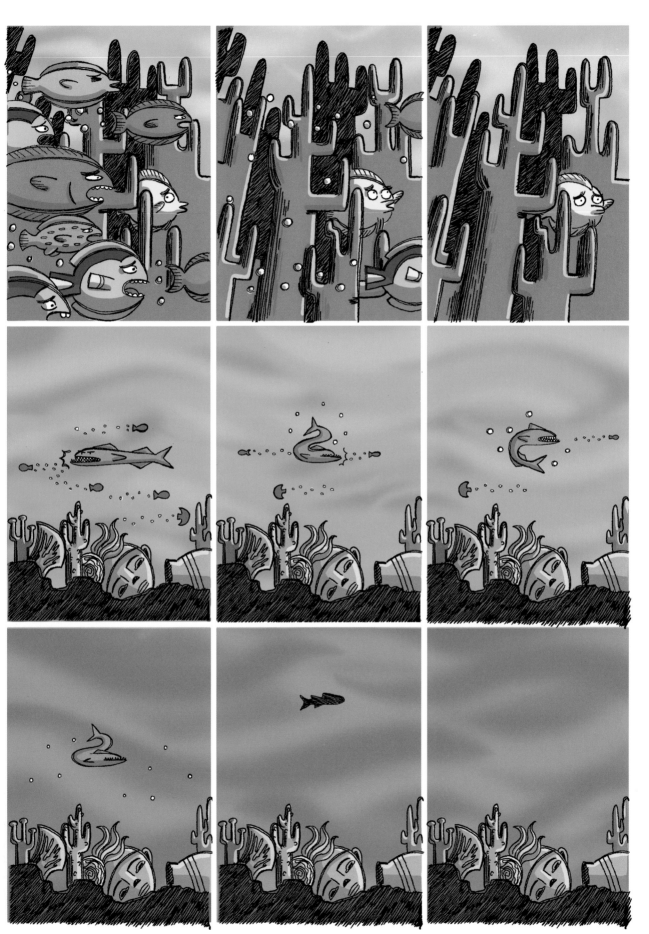

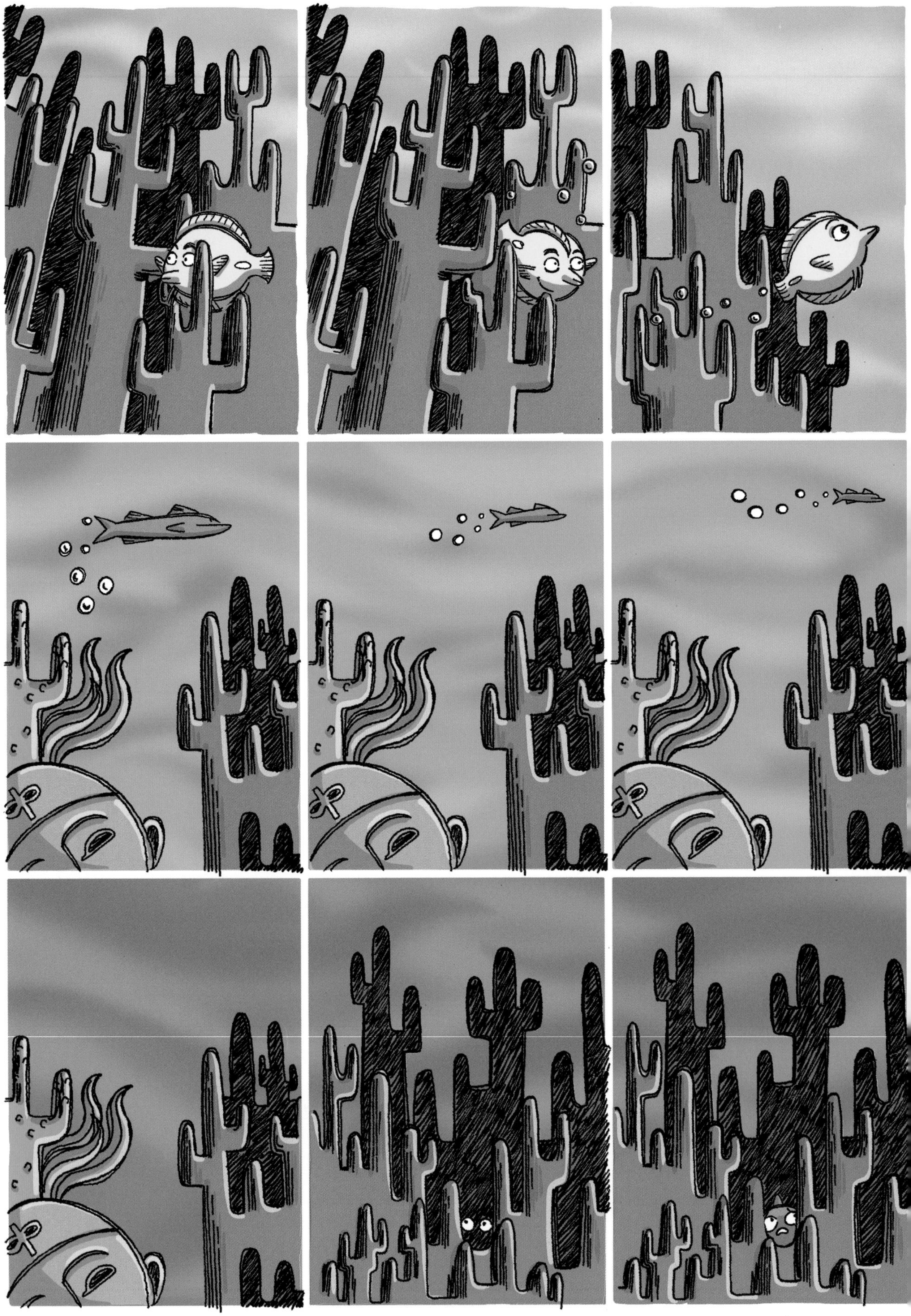

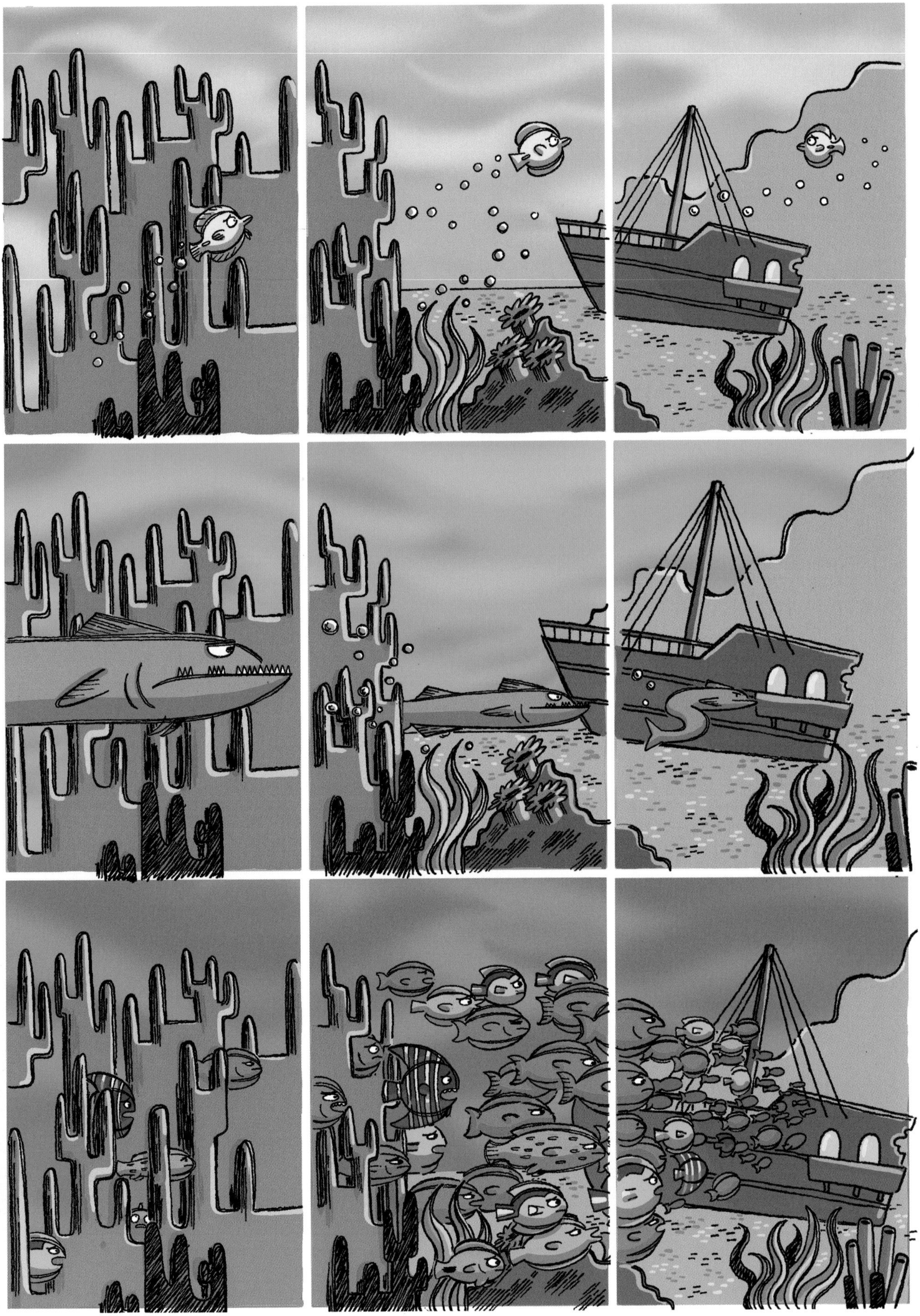

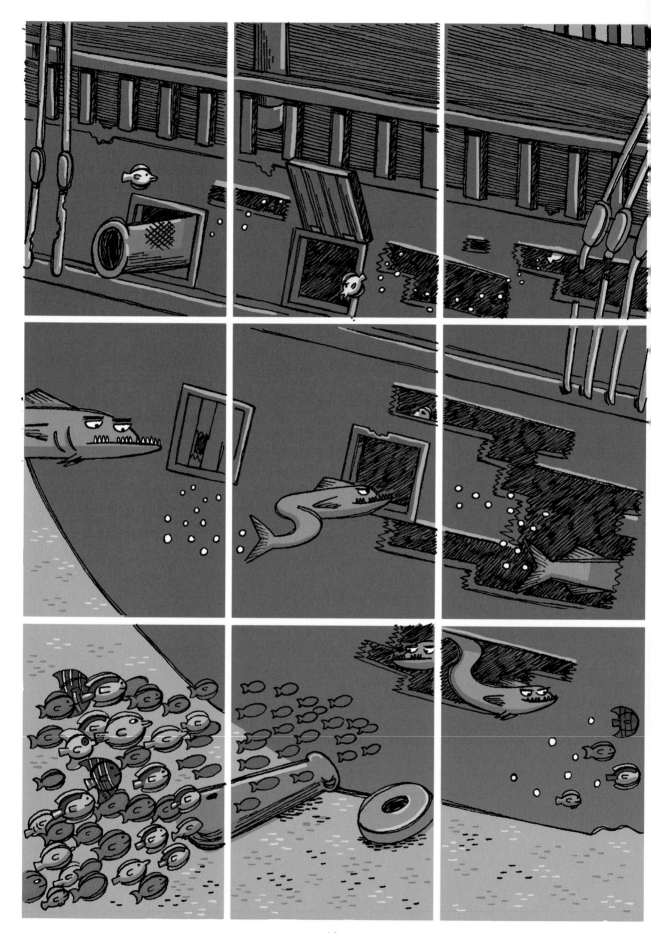

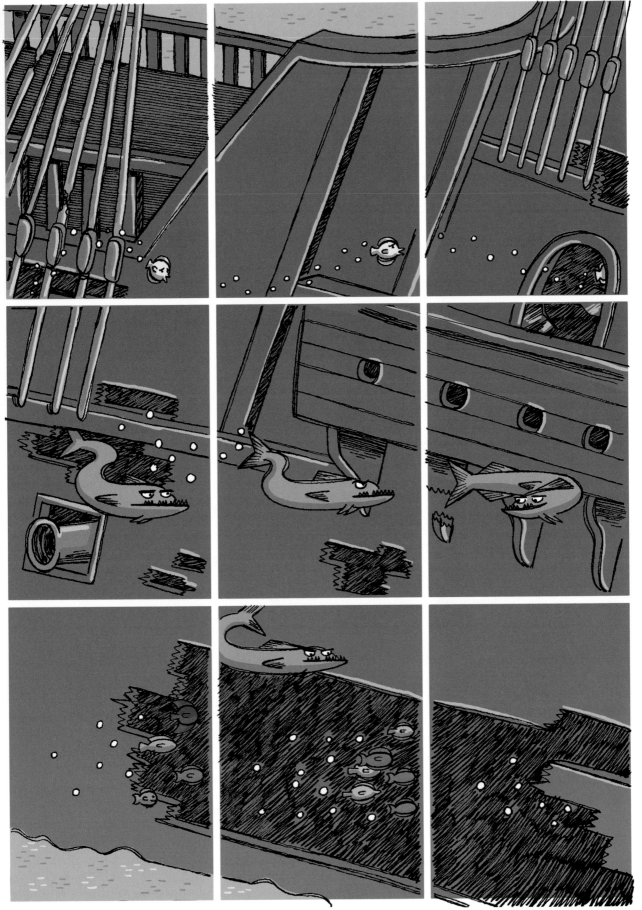

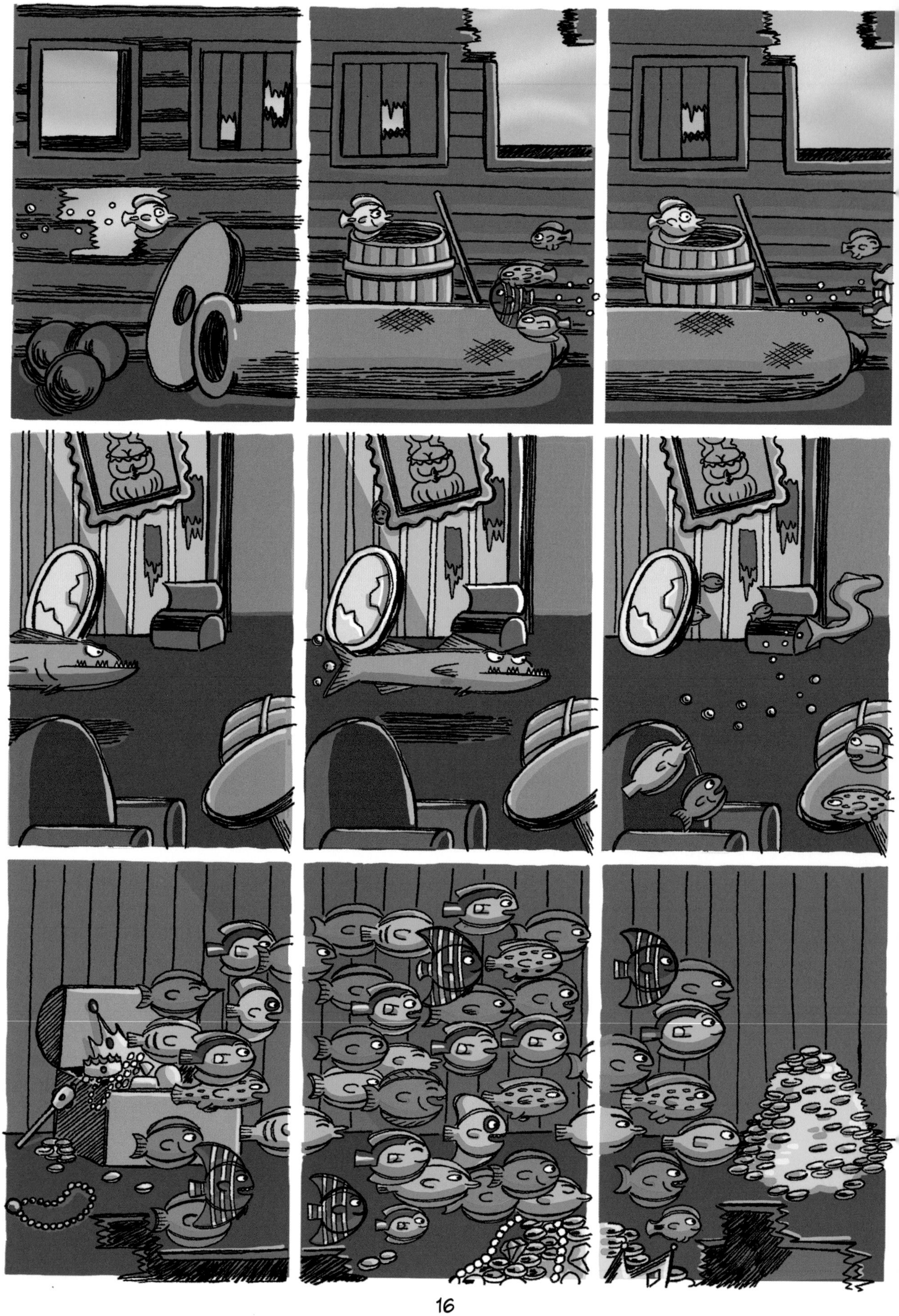

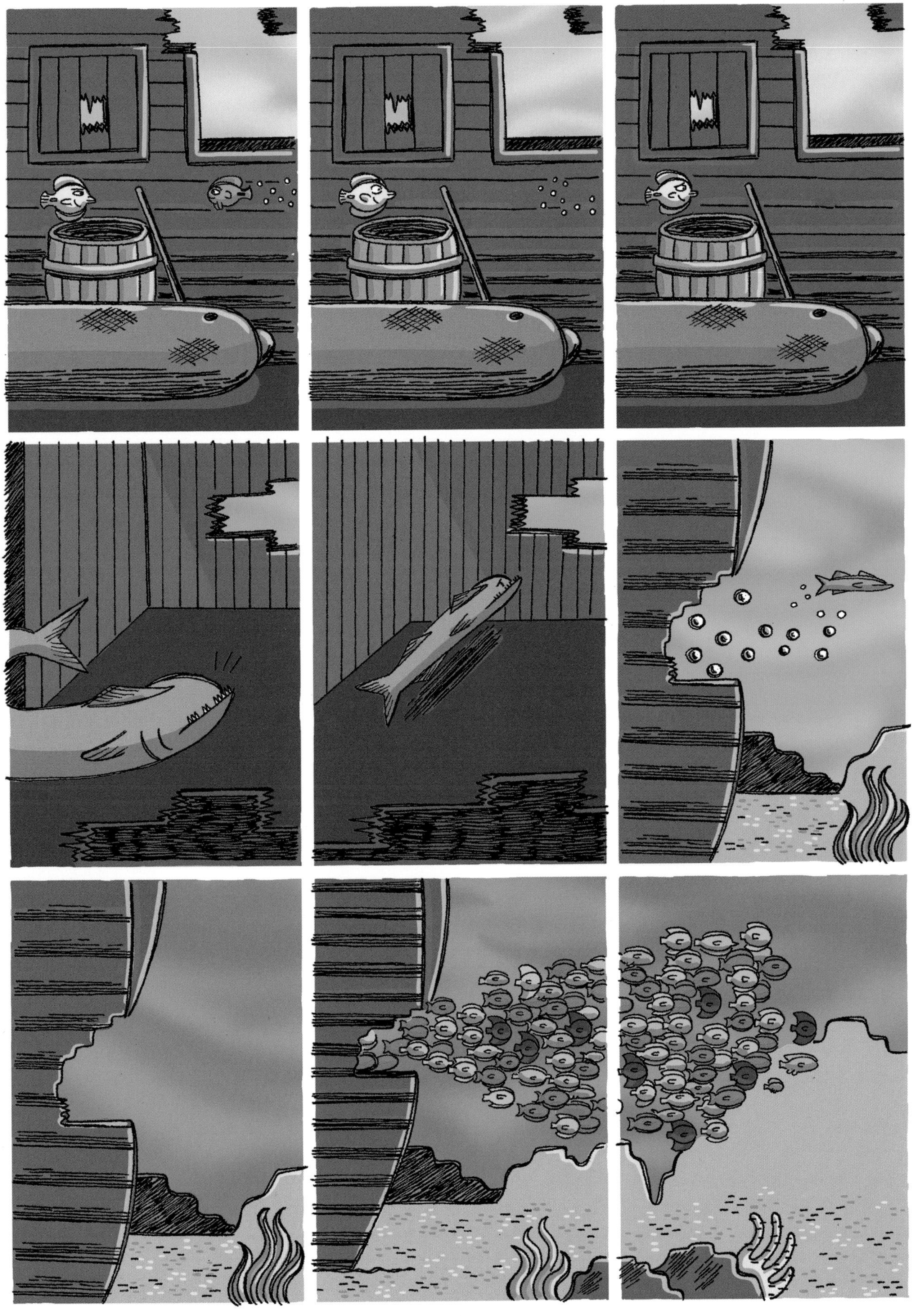

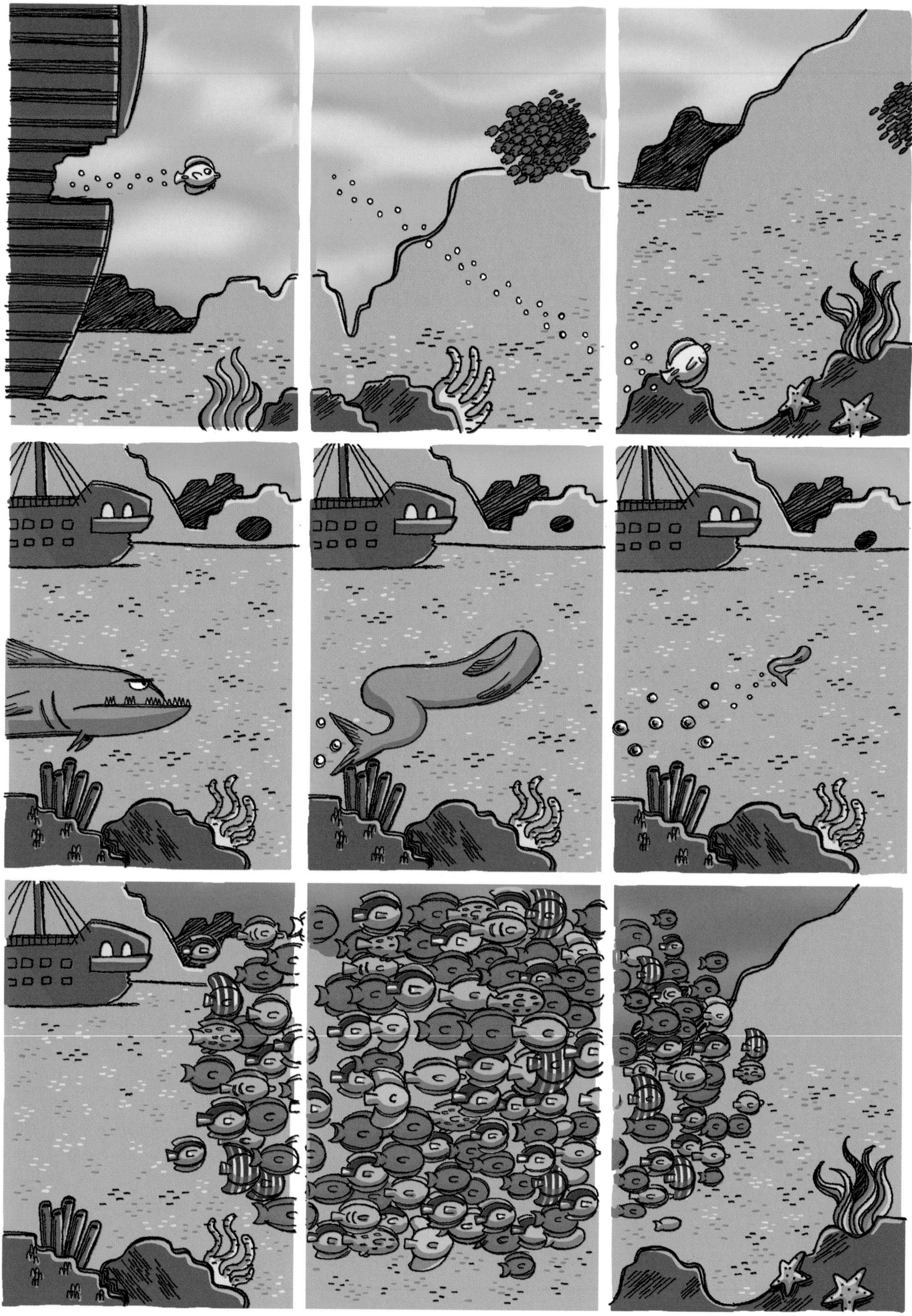

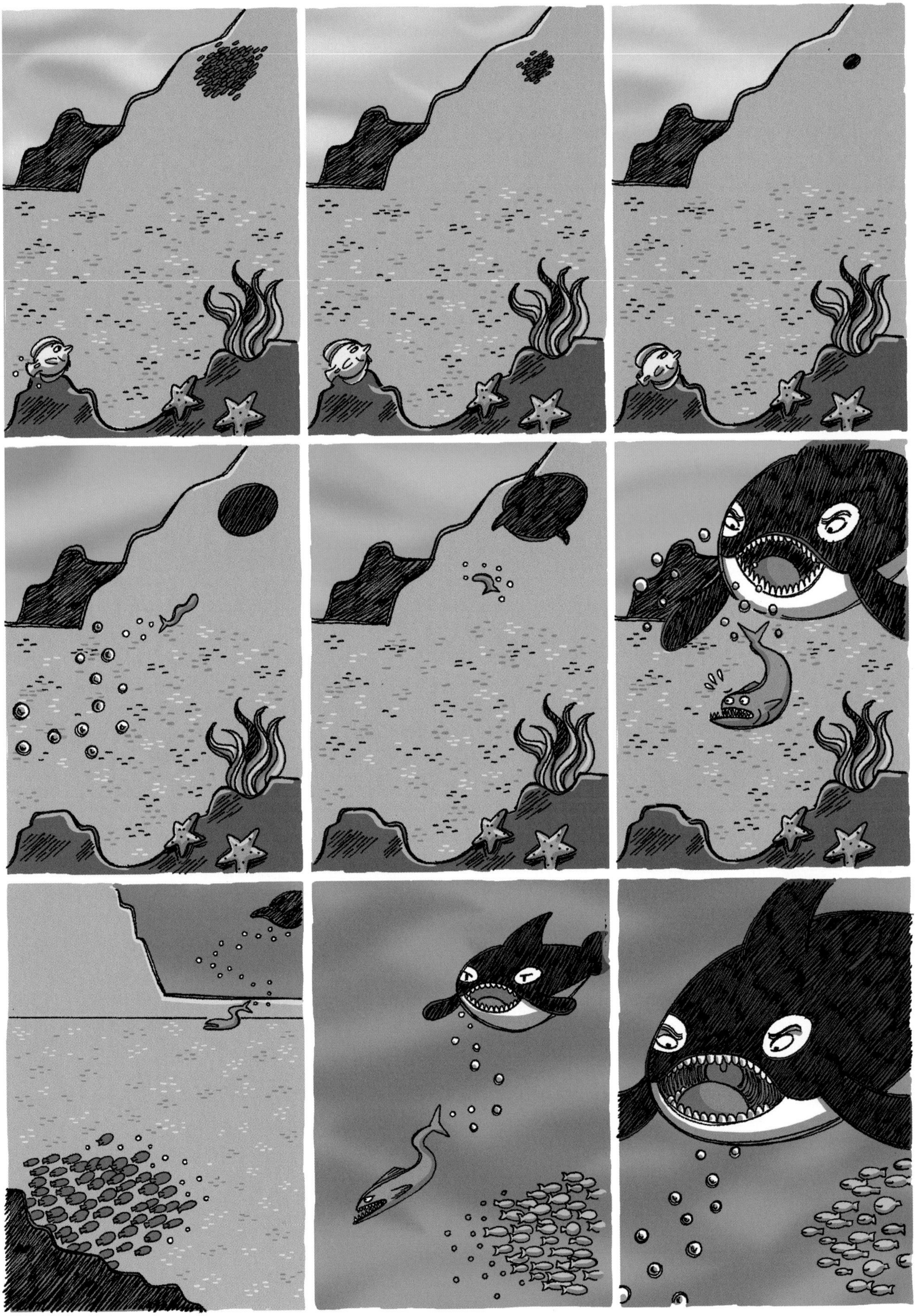

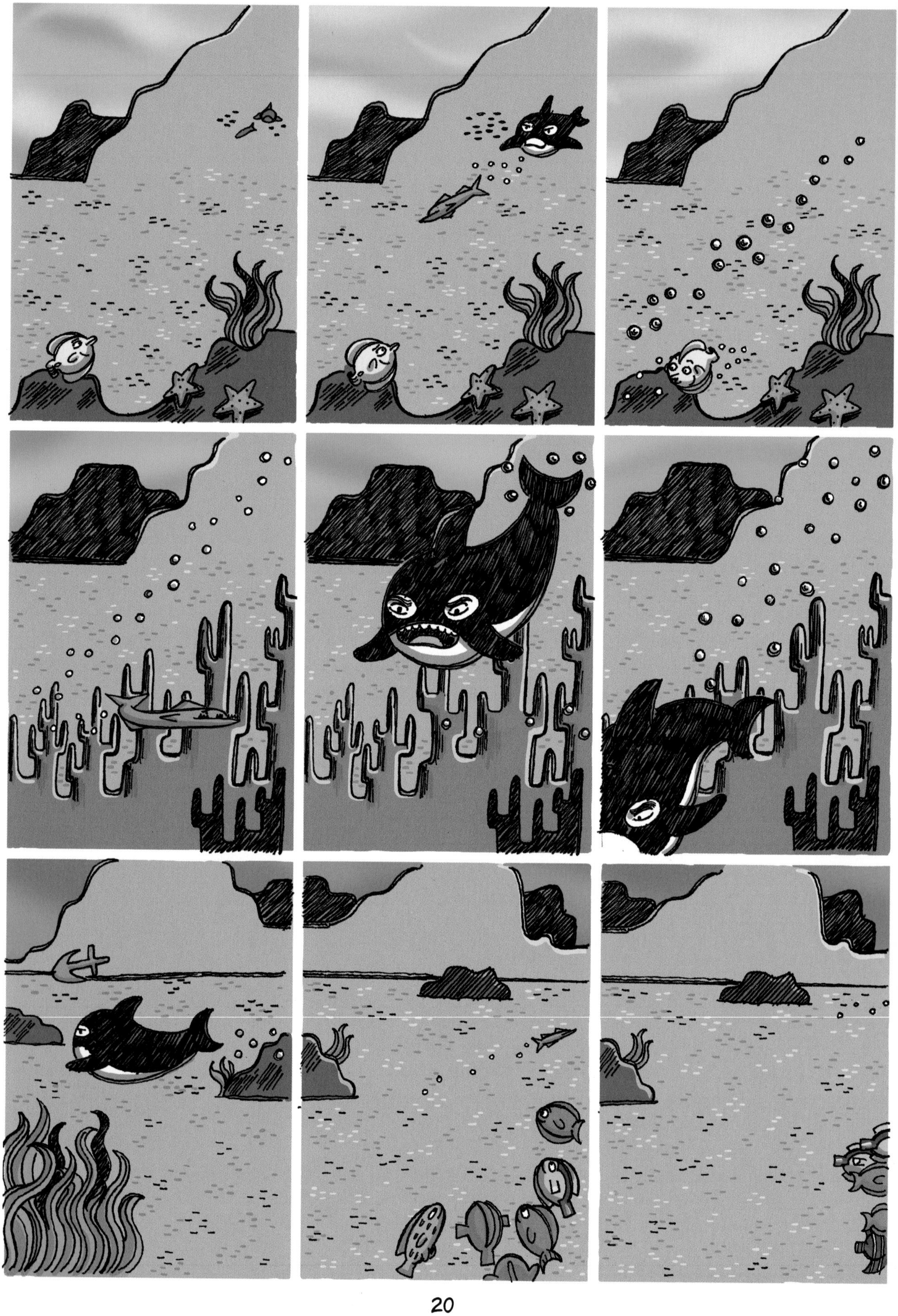

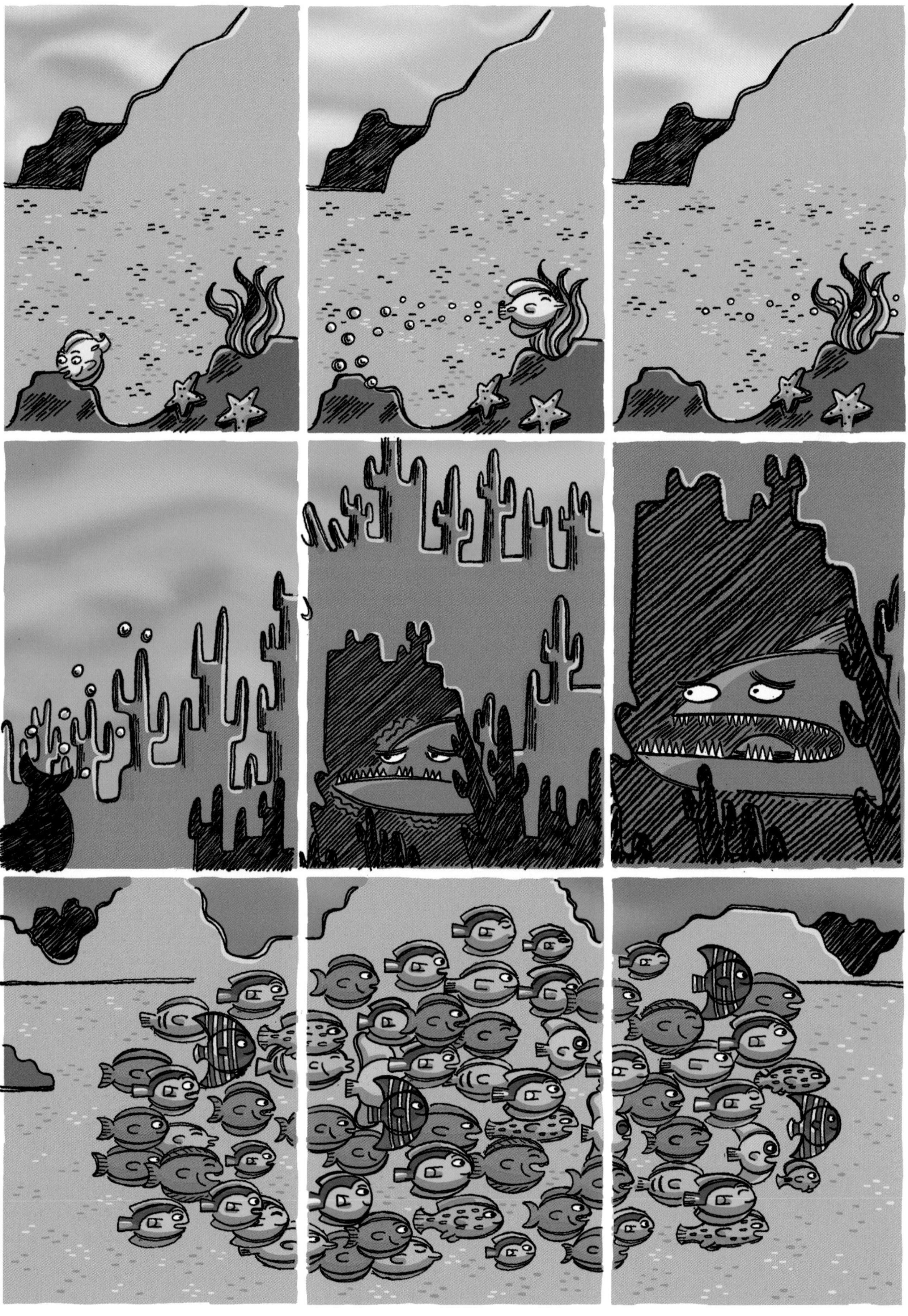

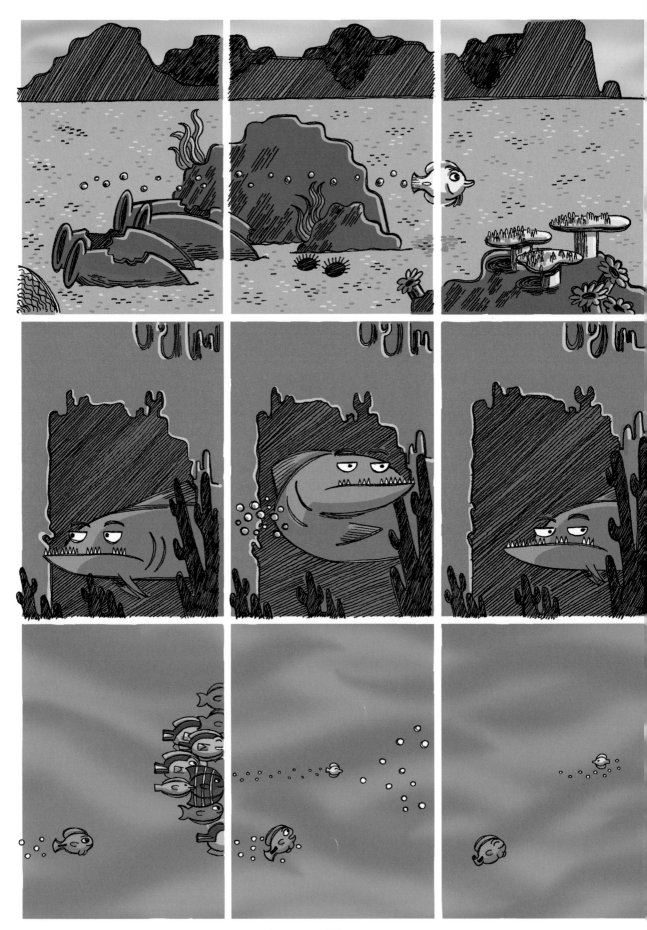

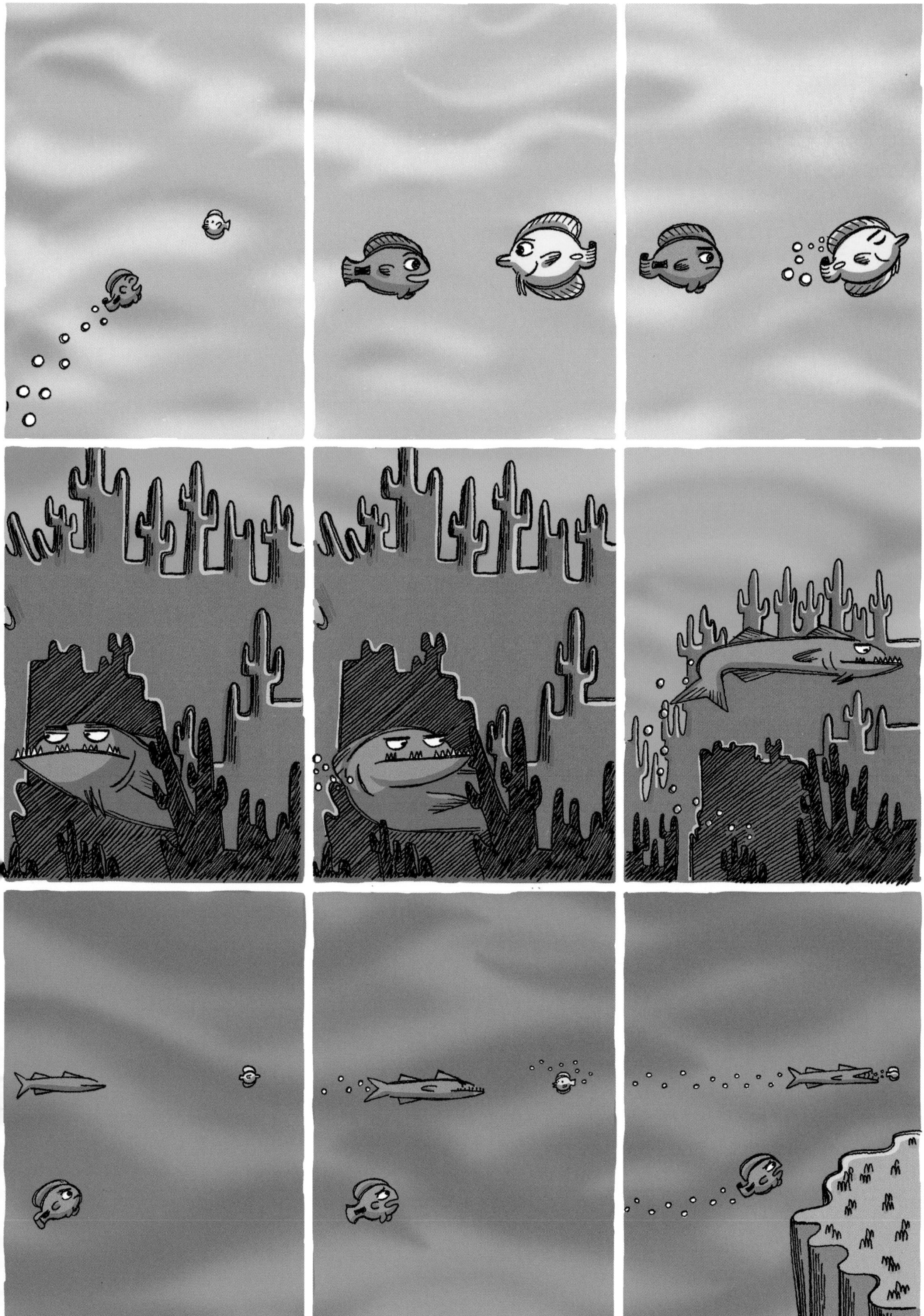

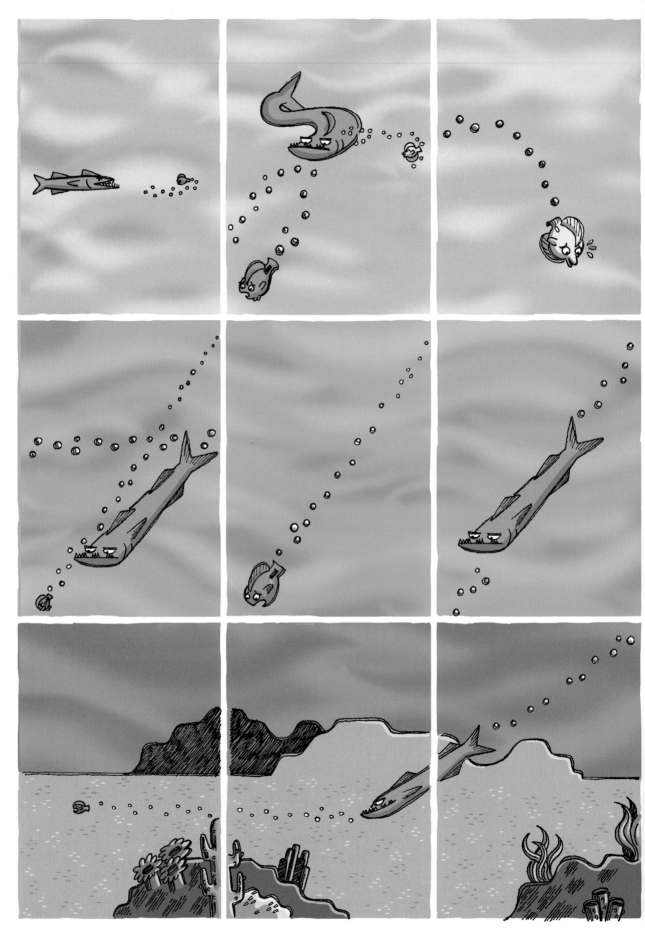

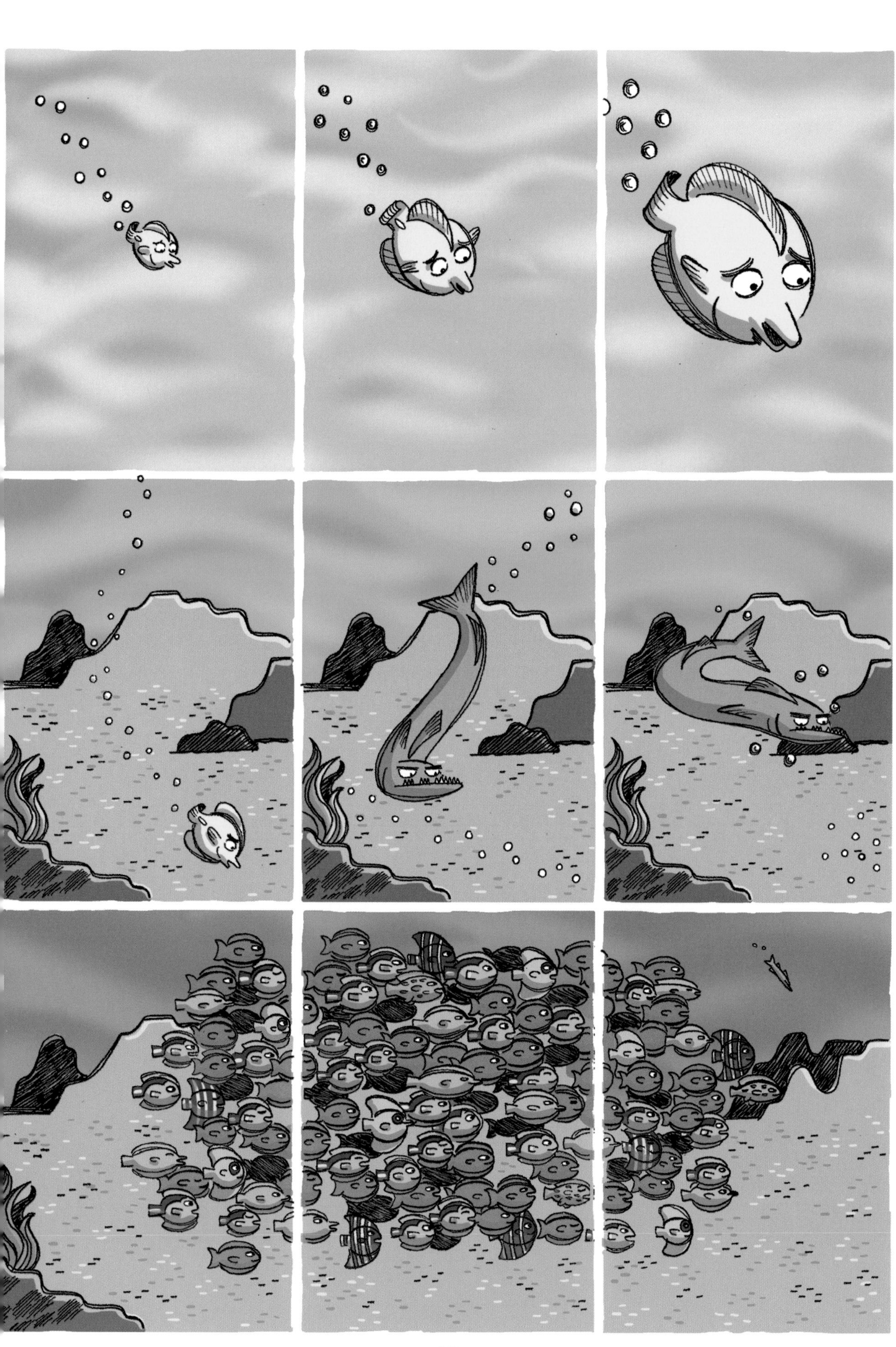

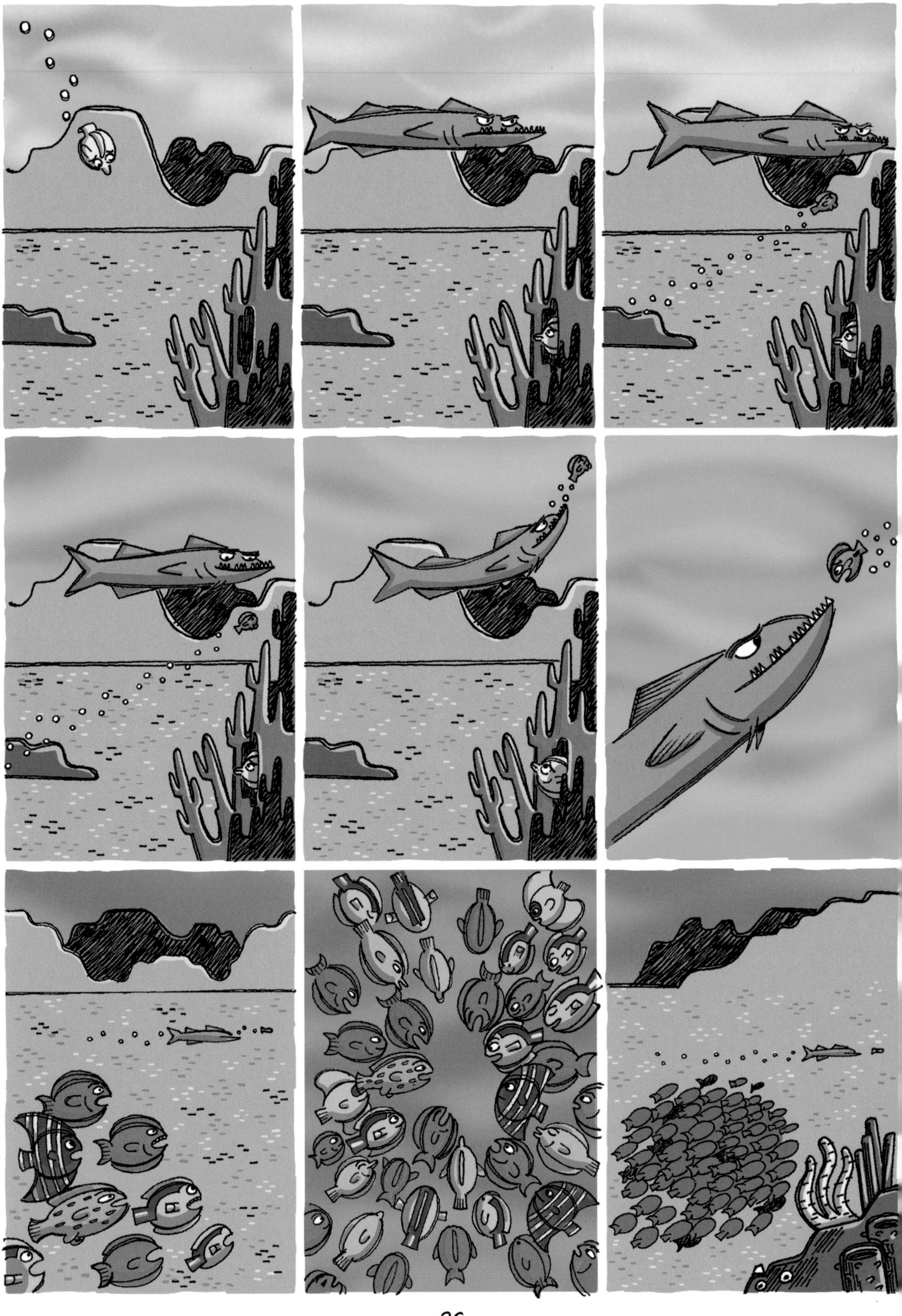

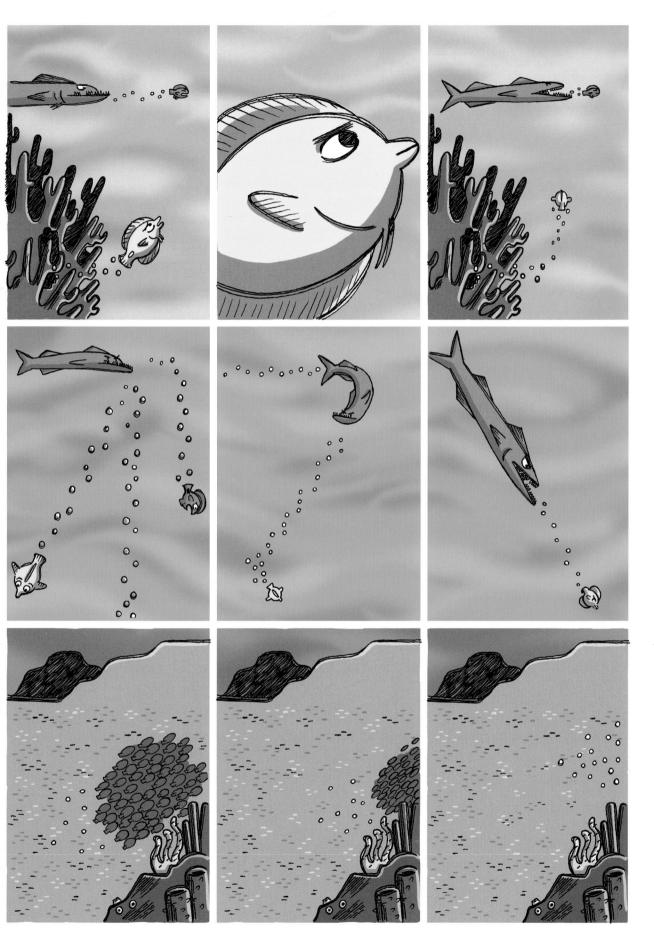

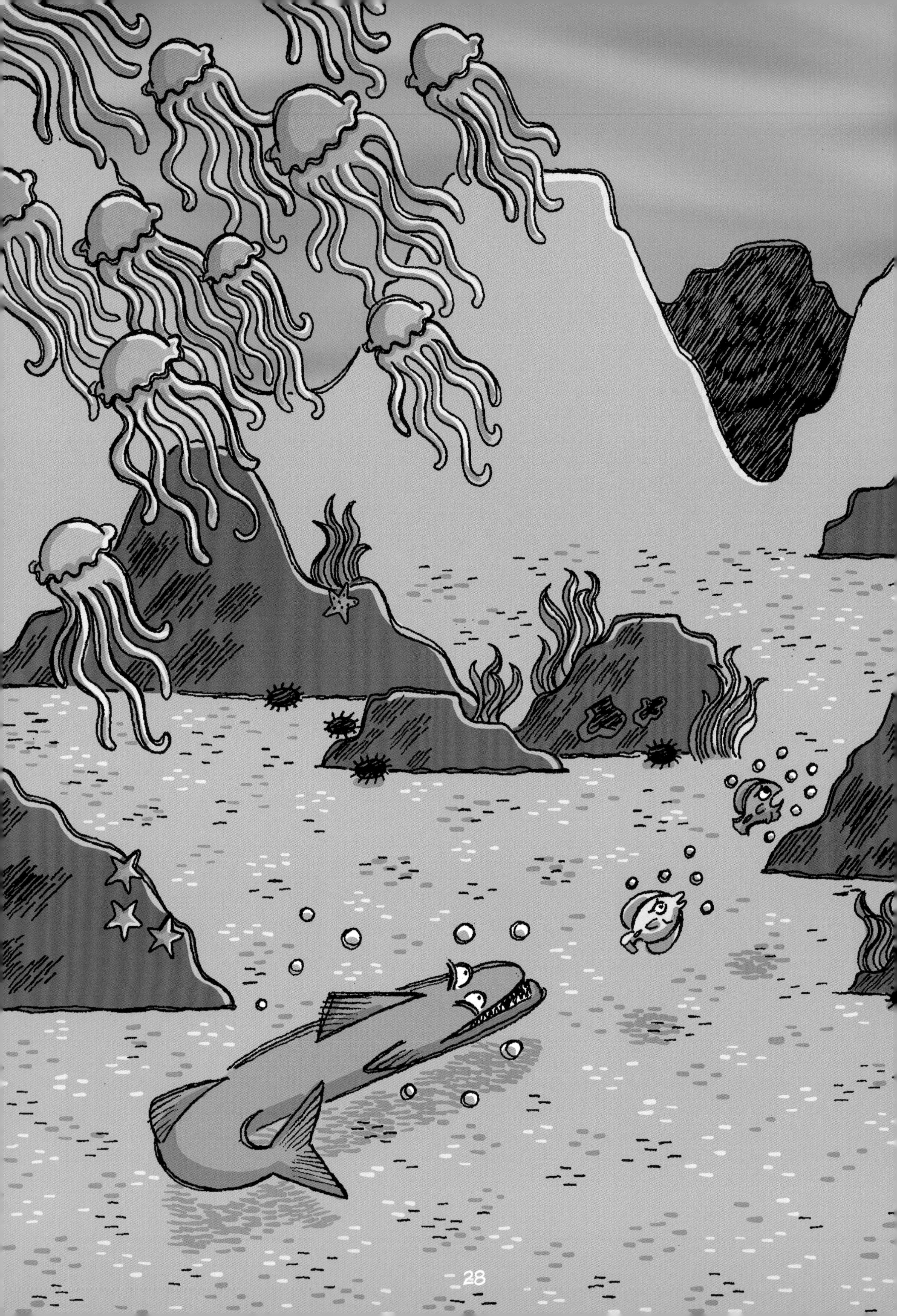

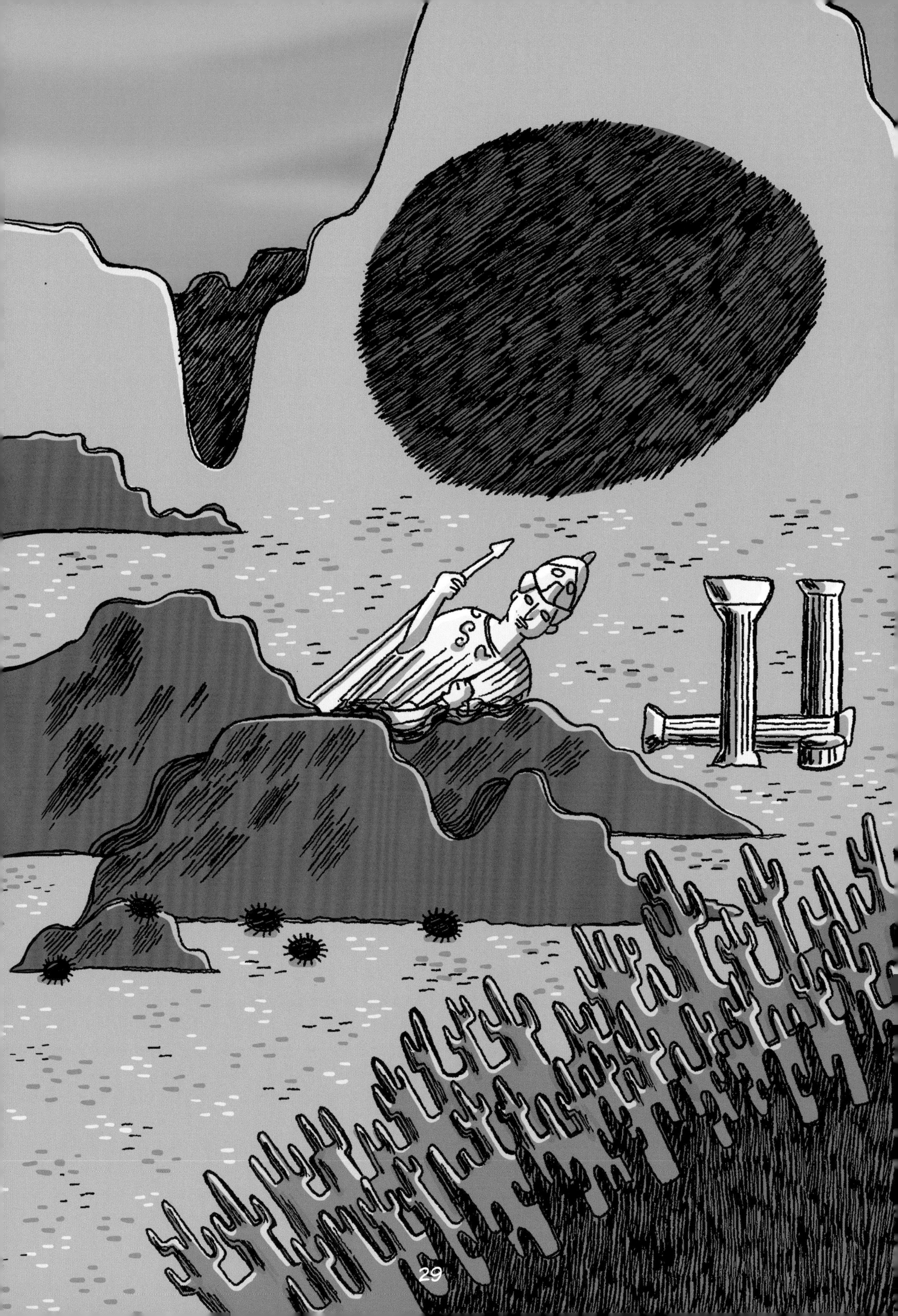

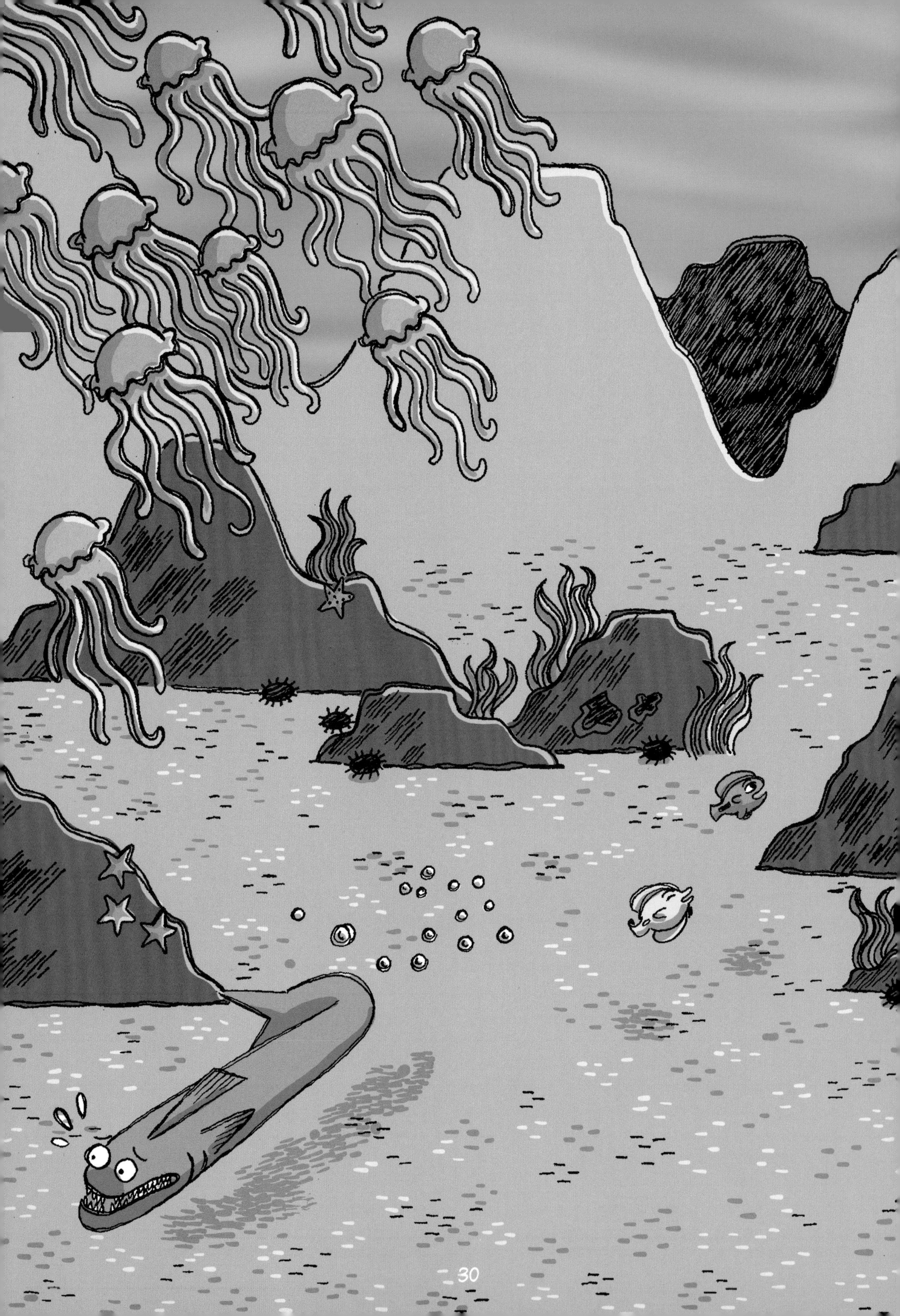

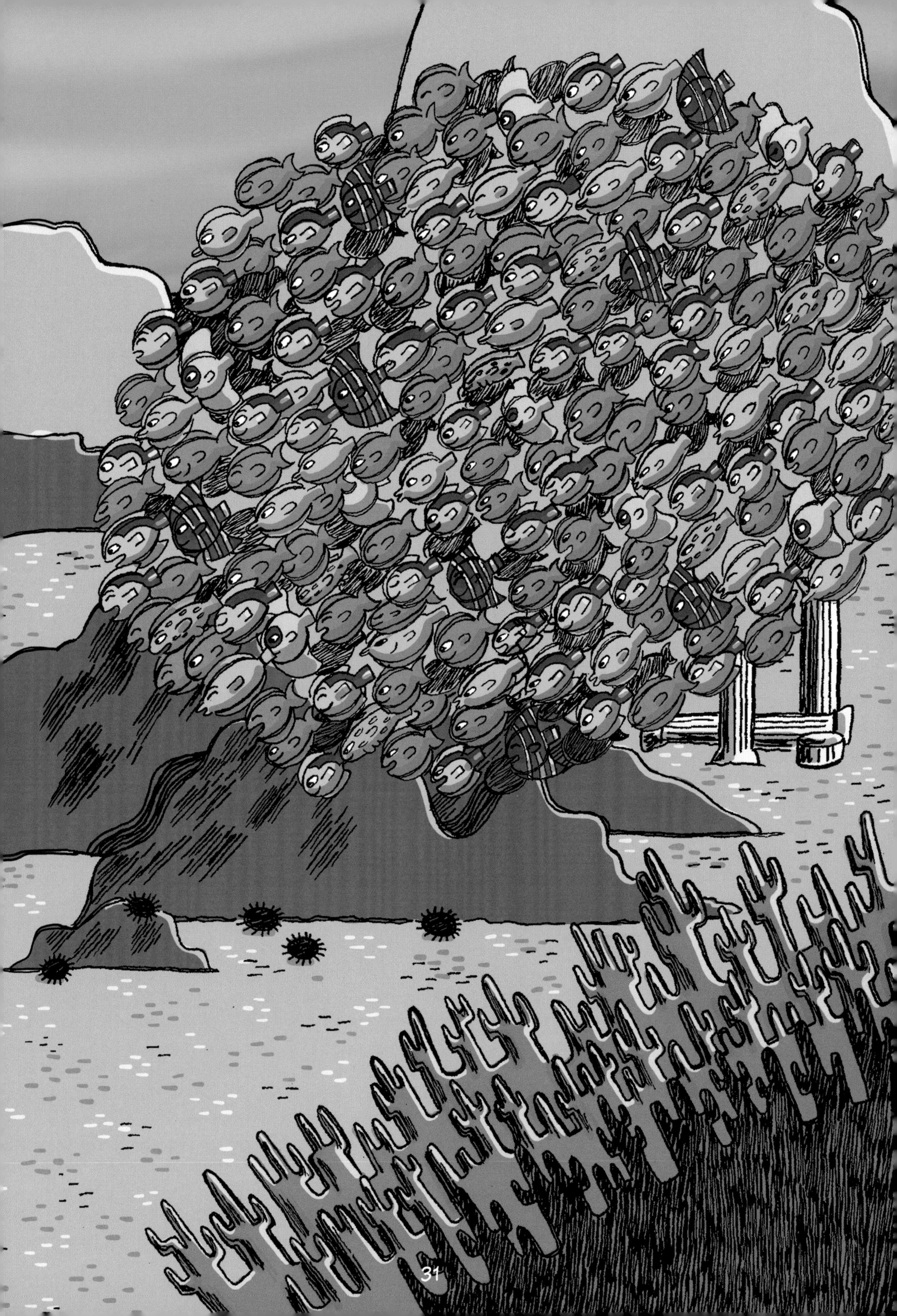

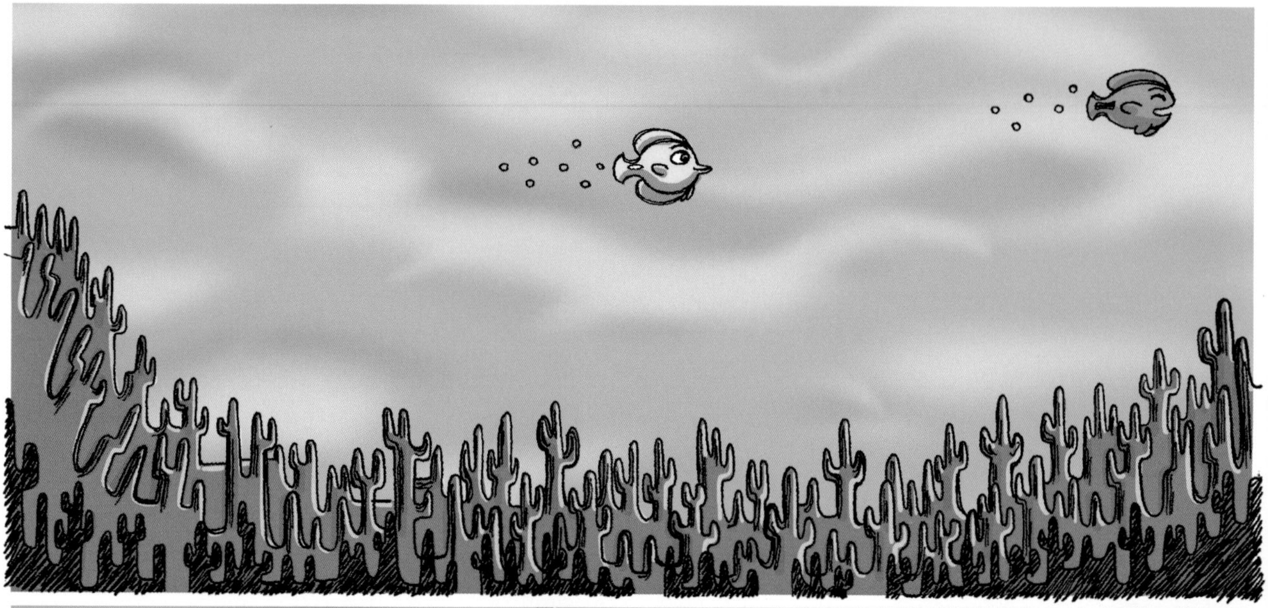
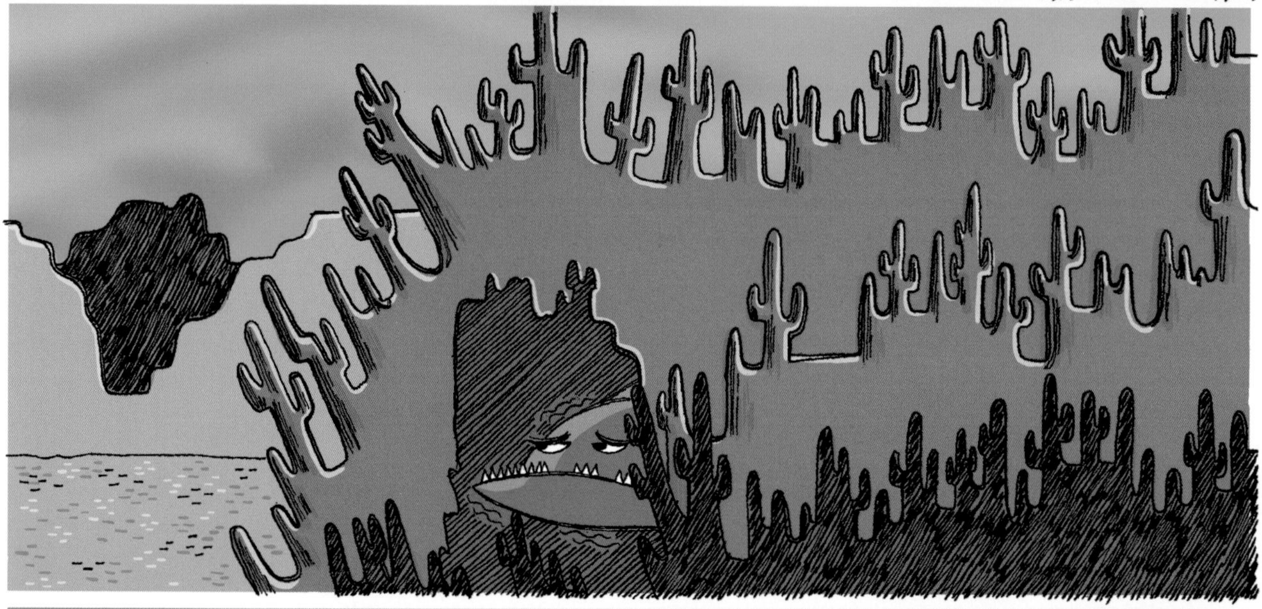
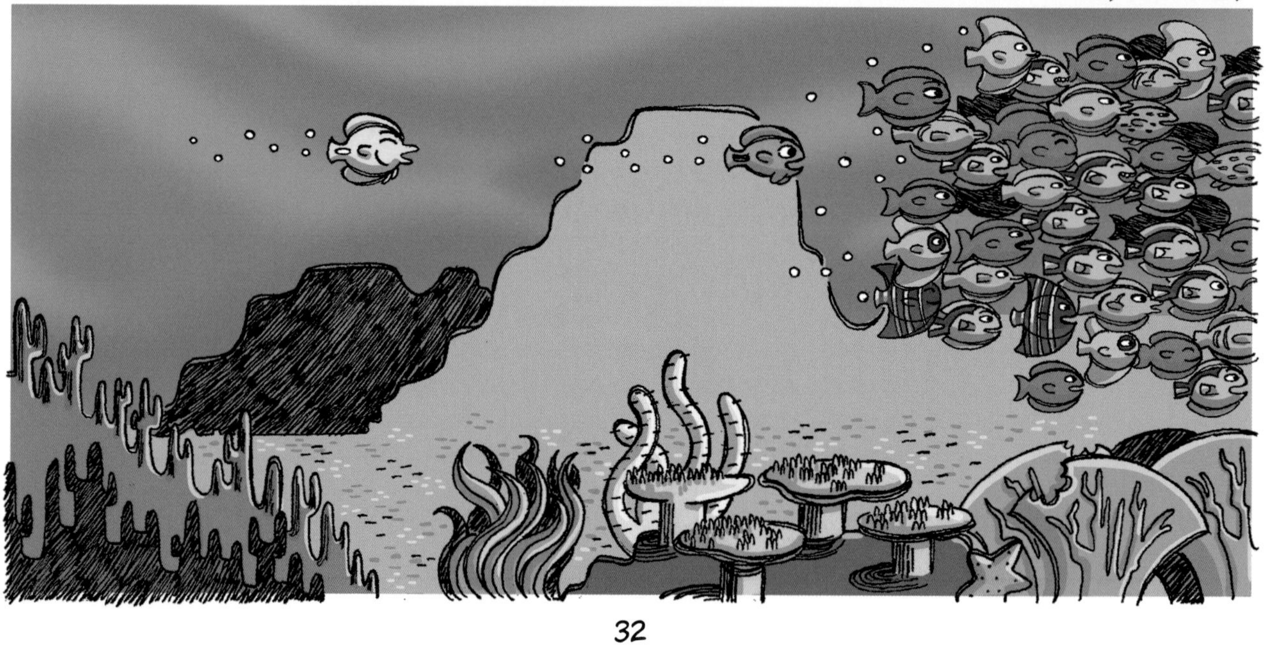

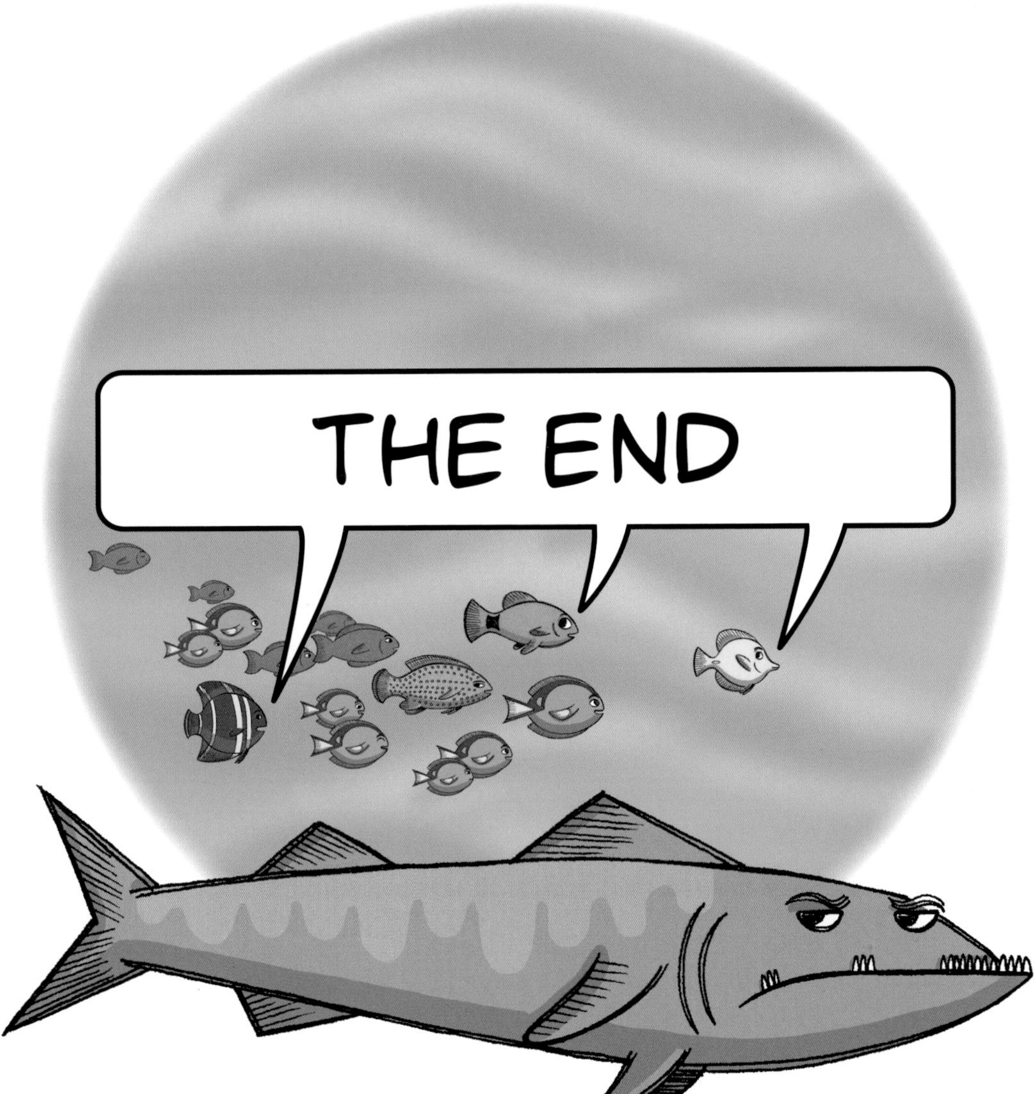
THE END

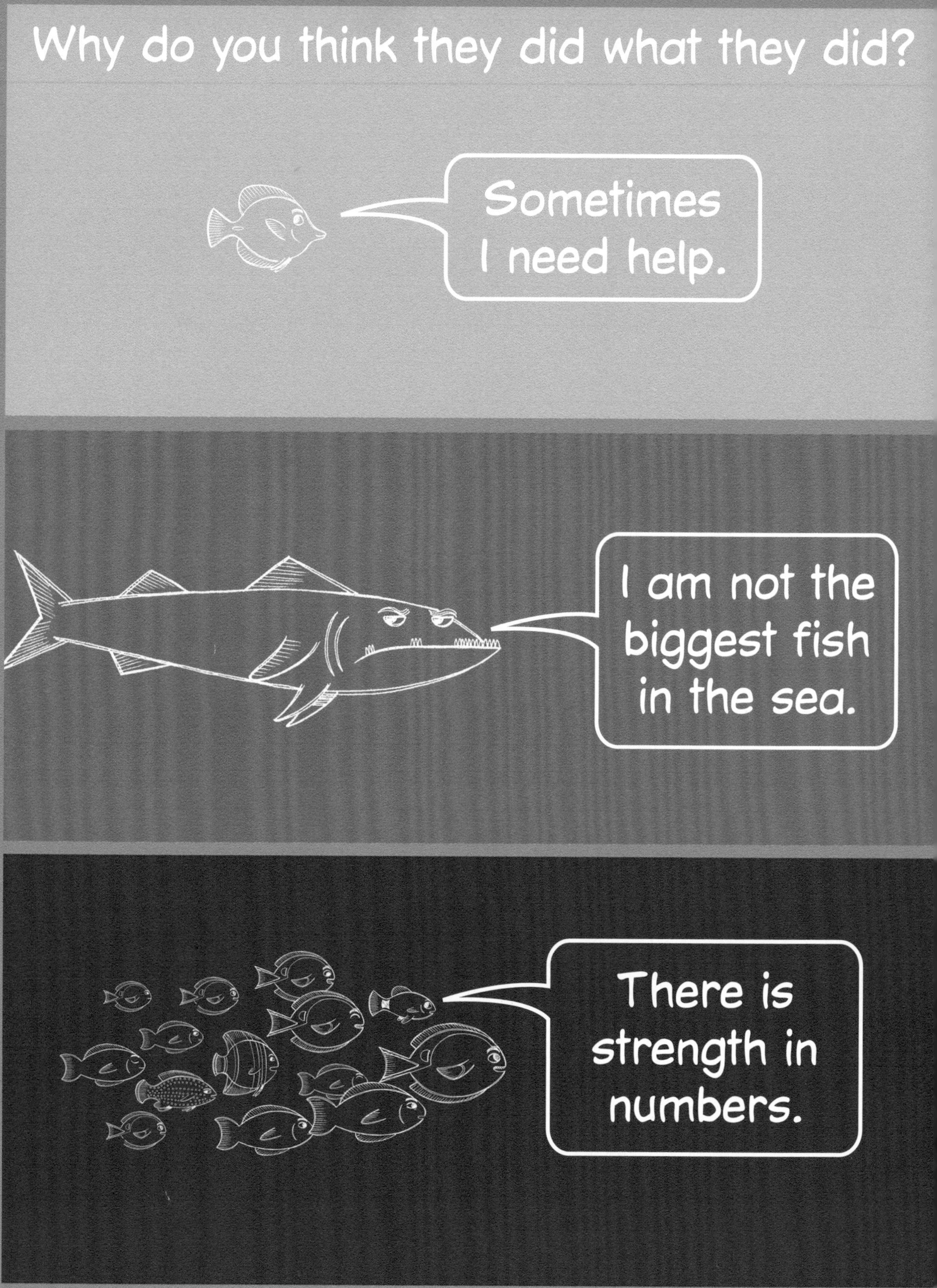
Why do you think they did what they did?
Sometimes I need help.
I am not the biggest fish in the sea.
There is strength in numbers.

Why do we see things so differently?